She was drowsy and closed her eyes for a few moments. When she opened them, she saw Daniel raise one hand and count on his fingers.

"What are you doing?"

"Counting the kisses I have given you."

"You will need two hands."

He rolled over and stroked her hair. "You looked so lovely lying there. I did not want to disturb your sweet slumber."

"Oh, please don't talk like that," she said, shielding her eyes from the sun and laughing.

"Are you completely awake?"

"Yes, why?"

"Never let it be said that I took advantage of a sleeping woman." He pulled her into his arms and kissed her quite passionately. Several times.

ROMANCE

BOOK YOUR PLACE ON OUR WEBSITE AND MAKE THE READING CONNECTION!

We've created a customized website just for our very special readers, where you can get the inside scoop on everything that's going on with Zebra, Pinnacle and Kensington books.

When you come online, you'll have the exciting opportunity to:

- View covers of upcoming books
- Read sample chapters
- Learn about our future publishing schedule (listed by publication month *and author*)
- Find out when your favorite authors will be visiting a city near you
- Search for and order backlist books from our online catalog
- Check out author bios and background information
- Send e-mail to your favorite authors
- Meet the Kensington staff online
- Join us in weekly chats with authors, readers and other guests
- Get writing guidelines
- AND MUCH MORE!

**Visit our website at
http://www.kensingtonbooks.com**

What He Doesn't Know

Lisa Noeli

ZEBRA BOOKS
KENSINGTON PUBLISHING CORP.
www.kensingtonbooks.com

ZEBRA BOOKS are published by

Kensington Publishing Corp.
850 Third Avenue
New York, NY 10022

All Kensington titles, imprints and distributed lines are available at special quantity discounts for bulk purchases for sales
promotion, premiums, fund-raising, educational or institutional
use.

Special book excerpts or customized printings can also be
created to fit specific needs. For details, write or phone the
office of the Kensington Special Sales Manager: Attn. Special
Sales Department. Kensington Publishing Corp., 850 Third
Avenue, New York, NY 10022. Phone: 1-800-221-2647.

Zebra and the Z logo Reg. U.S. Pat. & TM Off.

ISBN 0-8217-7818-8

First Printing: June 2005
10 9 8 7 6 5 4 3 2 1

Printed in the United States of America

For Kay Anders,
who supports the arts.

Chapter One

"Do be careful, sir," the stage manager whispered.

Nodding, Lord Daniel York tried to edge past an upended and amazingly round rump, encircled by a short, frilly skirt. He could not see the face of the rump's owner, who was bent over a box of battered dance shoes and searching through them.

Lord York, being an observant man in a narrow place, noted that her pink knitted drawers sagged a little around the ankles and that she wore almost nothing above the waist, save a scrap of pink gauzy material, carelessly tied around her back. She also sported an enormous wig, which moths had found tasty. He could see the net cap that held the artificial hair in place.

In her haste she tossed several shoes out upon the floor, and he stumbled over one.

Tom patted her rump. "Move over, Molly. Ye're blocking the way."

She didn't budge. Lord York looked around. There seemed to be no end to the backstage labyrinth and no other way out.

Molly continued to rummage through the box.

"Can't find me shoes, Tom." She sent a few more flying right and left. "Oh, well. I shall have to pinch a pair from someone." She straightened up and spied another pink-clad dancer, holding her shoes in one hand and sipping from an amber flask in the other.

"Naow, Molly," the stage manager said in a warning tone. "Remember the sixth commandment. Thou shalt not pinch."

"But Lucy won't notice. There's whiskey in that bottle, mark my words. She's drunk."

Readying for battle, Molly pulled up her knitted drawers as she stepped back, bumping into Lord York.

He pressed himself against the corridor wall as she threw him a coy look over her shoulder. "Hallo! Who's this?"

"A distinguished visitor," Tom said.

She wiggled her rump against Lord York and laughed. "Oo! How nice. We don't get too many of those. You look lonely, sir. P'raps I can help."

Lord York drew a deep breath, but he thought it best not to answer.

Molly turned around and let her body touch his again for a moment. He was not even remotely stirred. She eyed him curiously, adjusting her wig, which had slipped a bit. "Thanks ever so much, Tommy. I likes him."

Tom took her by the arm to drag her away, none too gently. "Mind yer manners. He has an appointment with Mr. Shy."

"Oh, right, the new slave driver. Not that anyfink has changed since Shy took over this poxy company. And when is he goin' to pay us, hey?"

"When the new show earns a profit," Tom said. "Now shut up, and act like a lady fer once."

"I am always a lady," she said indignantly, "in spite of hell."

A pair of stagehands came through, carrying a long ladder between them and pieces of painted felt over their shoulders. Lord York took advantage of the interruption to move away from Molly and Tom. The heavy tread of the stagehands did not muffle the sound of other footsteps behind him, light and sure.

He turned around. There was no one there. Molly was barefoot and Tom Higgins was standing still. Was he being followed? Whoever it was had a knack for staying out of sight.

Tom gave Molly a severe look. "Say ye're sorry. 'Tis right rude of ye to wiggle about in that wanton way and speak so forward to our distinguished visitor."

She put her hands on her hips and pouted. "Beggin' yer pardon, I'm sure. How was I to know his lordship prefers boys?"

"Molly, ye have gone too far!"

"Ow, shut yer gob. I was only joking. But I do want a rich man, Tom. Keep an eye out." She favored Lord York with a gap-toothed smile. "The landlady at the boarding house is screamin' for the rent, bangin' on me door at all hours. I'm gettin' circles under me eyes and losin' me youthful bloom."

Tom coughed in an exaggerated way.

"None of your sarcasm, Tommy Higgins. I don't have a shilling to me name and I am in dire straits."

"We all are," he muttered.

The dancer wiped away a nonexistent tear and heaved a theatrical sigh, looking for sympathy from Lord York instead. "The bitch threatened to put me and Nippy—that's me parrot—out on the street. I gave her a black eye, I did."

"The gentleman ain't interested in yer parrot."

"Are ye sure?" Molly looked hopefully at Lord York. "He is a fine bird, sir."

Tom steered her a little distance away and hissed in her ear. "He is here to see Mr. Shy, not buy a bloomin' parrot!"

"Tell him we want our money!" Molly called. Her eyes sparkled with mischief. She broke free of Tom's grip, and Lord York watched her warily.

"Ye are really very handsome," she said boldly, sidling closer. "Such long legs. And such a manly form. A noble sort o' nose too. And beautiful eyes. A luv'ly head of hair. I love to run me fingers through a man's hair and yers is nice and dark. And ever so silky." She came closer still. "Are yer teeth real?"

"That's enough!" Tom snapped.

She stuck out her tongue at the stage manager. "His lordship won't give us a smile and he hasn't said a word. I was curious, that's all."

She twirled a stray lock of her wig around one finger and batted her eyelashes. "Forgive me impertinence, sir. But I prefers natural choppers, especially in an older gentleman. Not that ye are old, of course."

Lord York merely nodded, nonplussed by Molly's unwelcome flirting and her odd questions. He kept his gaze fixed on her face, thinking that she had once been passably pretty.

Were she not wearing that moth-eaten wig, were her face not covered with thick white paint from her forehead to her chin and her blue eyes not bloodshot for God only knew what reason, she would be passably pretty still.

But working in the theater changed even the loveliest girls quickly, save for the few who became stars—and those fortunate ones glowed all too briefly. He felt a flash of pity for Molly.

Certainly she had missed her chance or perhaps had never had one at all. The hard expression on her face and the heavy stage makeup destroyed any illusion of beauty when seen so close. Still, Lord York managed a fractional smile.

"Behave yerself," Tom growled. "The gentleman is a lover of the arts."

"Fancy that. I do love a man who loves the arts." She smirked at Lord York, whose smile vanished. He could think of no response, and said nothing.

"I would be happy to demonstrate my terpsichorean skills for him. Oo! Just thinking about it makes me shiver!" She clasped her upper arms with both hands and rubbed imaginary goose bumps, causing her barely clad bosom to jiggle.

Lord York could not help but look, though he found the sight curiously unexciting.

She laughed again, more rudely than before. "What did you say your name was, ducks?" Molly left off rubbing her arms and tugged at the waistband of her pink drawers again, hitching them up rather inelegantly.

"He didn't say." Tom scowled. "And I shan't tell ye. Now cover up before ye catch cold, and be off." He picked up a large, paint-spattered piece of felt that the passing stagehands had dropped and put it over her shoulders.

Molly flung it to the floor with the hauteur of a duchess—a deeply offended duchess. Then she turned up her nose and sauntered away. She stopped to talk to the other dancer, taking a long swig from the bottle Lucy offered before handing it back.

"Sorry, sir. Molly does put on airs, considerin' she is only a nimp."

"A what?" Lord York found his voice at last.

"A nimp. You know, a lady of the Greekian forest. All the rage with the bucks and the blades, the nimps are. And the sadders likewise."

"The who?"

"The sadders—you know, the hairy blokes that chases the nimps."

Understanding dawned and Lord York smiled. "Ah, yes. Nymphs and satyrs. Educated theatergoers will enjoy a classical touch, I am sure."

Tom nodded. "Exactly. The nimps and sadders are all from the chorus and used to going about nearly naked."

"I see," said Lord York, a little stiffly. He had not been informed that his first venture into theatrical production would involve naked performers. He made a mental note not to send free tickets to his Methodist aunt. "And what do they do?"

"Oh, prance about," Tom said cheerfully. "The nimps bang tambourines and make a racket in case the play caused anyone to fall asleep. Then the sadders chase them and try to pull their clothes off. It is a most edifyin' spectacle."

"Indeed."

"The rehearsals commence today, sir. You can watch if you like."

"Thank you. Perhaps I will. But I seem to remember that our proposed play had nothing to do with ancient Greece. Was it not set in a fashionable London drawing room?"

"It was, yes," Tom said cautiously.

Lord York raised an eyebrow. "Where is it set now? Are there naked nimps—nymphs—in it?"

"Course not. They can never remember lines. Naow, the Drury Lane Company beat us to the drawing room, is all. They are offerin' a sophisticated comedy of manners. *Cupid and the Countess,* I believe it is called. So we decided to cancel *The Mistress of Mayfair* and do *The Shepherdess* instead. It is a rustic love story."

"I am not familiar with that play," Lord York said.

"Hasn't been written yet. Our dramatist is working on it. Would ye like to meet him?"

"Certainly."

"We gave him an office upstairs. Makes him feel important and he can't hurt anybody. Temperamental fellow, he is."

Tom led Lord York down another corridor, and they climbed a spiral staircase to the next level. Lord York looked behind him. He had heard light footsteps again—he was sure of it. But there was no one there.

"Tell you what really sets him off—doin' things over. He thinks every word he scribbles ought to be chiseled in white marble for eternity. He takes himself far too serious."

"That may be all to the good, Higgins. Drama should be serious."

Tom only shrugged. "It don't sell tickets."

"Is that the only consideration?"

The stage manager gave him a disbelieving look. "We must offer a full programme, sir. The public wants their pantomimes and dancing girls and Italian acrobats and mathematically gifted horses. That means a five-hour show."

"Dear me. Where does it begin and how does it end?"

They had reached the top of the staircase and proceeded to a closed door. Tom rapped upon it. "With Hugh Newsome, our resident genius." He opened the door.

"I heard that," the dramatist grumbled. "If I am a genius, I am insufficiently appreciated." He closed an old folio of plays and balanced a sheaf of paper on top of it, which immediately slid off and scatted over the floor. "Damnation! Everything and everyone is against me!"

"Calm yerself, Mr. Newsome," Tom said patiently. "Is there anyfink I can get fer ye? A nice new pen? A secondhand dictionary? What does it take to make a writer happy?"

"Money," Hugh retorted.

"Well, there's precious little of that around," Tom said. "This here is Lord Daniel York, by the way. He might be investing in this production and the theater."

The dramatist's expression brightened immediately.

"Sir, you appear to be a man of culture. I created a farce of matchless sophistication. Is it fair that it is removed from the bill simply because Drury Lane is offering something similar? Is it fair that I am asked to write a completely new play *and* compose love songs for country bumpkins whose greatest talent is herding sheep?"

"I cannot say," Lord York murmured. It was clear that the dramatist was prone to hysterics. He had no wish to encourage him.

Hugh ran a pudgy hand through his hair, which was already standing on end. "I find it infuriating! There were seventeen enchanting new musical numbers in *The Mistress of Mayfair* and now I must start over! Did Tommy mention that I am a lyricist? I tell you, I am insufficiently appreciated!" He gestured wildly and knocked over a stack of books that had been haphazardly piled behind his chair.

Tom examined his dirty fingernails nonchalantly. "Aye, he is, sir."

"Well then . . . to the tavern! Would you care to join me, Lord York? I find that yelling makes me thirsty."

"Thank you but no."

"I meant no offense, sir."

"None taken. Pray continue, Mr. Newsome."

The dramatist gave him an implorng look. "Could you ask Shy to increase my fee? I should not have to beg."

Lord York nodded politely. "It is a reasonable request. I shall discuss the matter with him."

"Thank you." Newsome frowned.

"Mr. Shy was askin' for the new pages, Hugh. The players need to start learnin' their lines. Have you done 'em?"

"Yes, yes, It is easy enough to write for rustics. Not as though they talk in polished epigrams. But I am not bitter. No, I have bid adieu to my beautiful bon mots and wonderful witticisms." Newsome gathered up the scribbled pages of the new play and thrust them at Tom. "These are the first two scenes, ready to go to the copyist. Please see that the original is returned to me, with a clean copy for my own use."

"When will you finish?" Tom asked. "We all wants to know how it turns out. Mr. Shy said to tell you that he is agog with anticipation."

"Agog, is he? Damn him! I will be finished when I am done!" Newsome bellowed.

"What?" Tom said, giving him a baffled look.

"I am waiting for in-spi-ra-tion," the dramatist said through his teeth. "Not that a stage manager would know what that word means. You seem to think that I just crank it out."

"But you do just crank it out, Hughie. Mr. Shy says that you go through pens and paper like they grows on trees."

Newsome pounded the desk with a pudgy fist. "He has no respect for the creative artist! And don't call me Hughie!"

"Mr. Shy did get the one and only Lizzie Louder-

milk to sign on for *The Shepherdess*," Tom pointed
out. "She'll make your songs sound twice as good
as they are. All of London will be hummin' yer
catchy little ditties."

"You are right about Lizzie, I suppose."

Tom nodded. "I'm always right."

"Miss Loudermilk is extraordinarily talented,"
Lord York began, "and deservedly popular. But I
must confess I did not quite understand what part
she might play in an elegant farce."

Hugh Newsome snorted. "Nor did I. But she is
perfect for rustic comedy. She is six feet tall in
stockings and has a voice that carries to the top-
most gallery. Not to mention that ghastly red hair."

"Don't forget her gigantical bosom," Tom said
with a huge grin. "A very fine sight it is." The
thought made him sigh with admiration.

The dramatist picked up a quill and nibbled on
it thoughtfully. "I must create a strapping blacksmith to play opposite her. A man of few words
and great strength. Someone who will make her
seem delicate and feminine."

"Ah, ye're missing the point. Lizzie is magnificent
just as she is. Many men appreciate a queenly lady."

"Well, they will have plenty of opportunity to appreciate Lizzie," Hugh said. "She is onstage most
of the night, per her contract. But not for the
dancing, of course."

Lord York smiled slightly. "I cannot imagine Miss
Loudermilk as a nymph."

The stage manager nodded his agreement. "Our
Lizzie is too dignified and too famous to scamper
about banging a tambourine. And the costume
would not flatter her majestic dimensions."

"Well said, Tom. Mr. Newsome, it has been most
interesting. I look forward to future discussions."

"Quite. Thank you for coming by. And Tom, I *would* like that secondhand dictionary."

"Very good, sir. I will send one of the lads to fetch it straightaway."

Another climb up a different staircase brought them to the next level and out into a more open area backstage. A group of dancers were chatting, identically dressed in pink knitted drawers, frilly skirts, and wigs like Molly's.

Lord York looked into the wings, noting the painted scenery flats that could be moved in tracks along the floor; and then looked above at the cavernous ceiling into the flies, where the backdrops were hung. There were many, each tied to a long pole that ran the length of the stage, and counterweighted with sandbags in strategic places.

"Hoi! Who's up there?" Tom shouted. He waved to a small man with black hair and a pointed mustache who balanced nimbly on the backdrop poles, hopping from one piece of rigging to another.

A dancer called, "Signor Arlecchino is installin' the new drops. We was afraid to watch. Most likely he'll break his bloody neck," she added, not without compassion.

That was a distinct possibility, Lord York thought. The man was at least forty feet above the stage.

"We bought sets and costumes from an Italian opera company as what was returning to Naples," Tom said. "They seem to have thrown in Signor Arlecchino as well. I wonder if he speaks English. Hoi! You there!"

"Hallo! Hallo!" the small man called back.

Tom grinned. "Well, p'raps he does. Arly, could you show us one of the drops?"

"*Si, si,*" Arlecchino said excitedly. "Which one you wants?"

"Is there a scene with sheep?"

"*Si,* the sheep. I have the sheep."

High overhead, he tugged on a rope or two, released several sandbags, and let a huge piece of painted canvas unfurl. Tom and Lord York jumped back just in time. The bottom of the backdrop hit the stage with a thump, raising a cloud of dust.

Tom waved the dust away from his face and let out a prodigious sneeze. Lord York pulled out a handkerchief and covered his nose and mouth. When the cloud of dust settled, both men found themselves staring at a dramatic depiction of a fully rigged man-of-war, cannons blazing, rolling on a stormy sea.

"Battlesheep," the man called. "It is very fine, no? Perhaps you have a play with the pirates."

"No, Signor Arlecchino. We need sheep, not a ship." Tom looked up into the flies. "Sheep are animals. Woolly, stupid animals."

"Perhaps if we made a noise like a sheep," Lord York murmured. He cleared his throat, feeling a little foolish. "*Baaa,*" he said. "*Baaa.*"

A faint sound of feminine mirth made him turn around, but all he saw was a moving bump in the heavy curtain drawn to one side of the proscenium arch. He glimpsed a pair of slender feet in white silk slippers beneath the curtain, but they quickly disappeared.

Ah. So someone *was* following him. But why? For the moment, he put the question out of his mind and *baaaed* again, a little more loudly.

Tom joined in. "*Baaaa! Baaaa!* Do you understand, Arly?"

"*Si, si! Le pecore!*"

"Is that what you call them?"

"Yes!" The man moved fearlessly from pole to pole high above, looking through the furled backdrops. "But we have no sheeps. I am so much sorry. Perhaps I paint some for you."

"Not today." Tom gestured toward the man-of-war backdrop. "Now roll this up. We need the stage. Rehearsal starts in an hour, ladies."

Signor Arlecchino obliged as Tom and Lord York crossed the apron and walked through a carved door built into the proscenium.

"Mr. Shy ought to be in his office. I know he is expectin' ye," Tom said.

"Very well."

They made their way down another corridor—this one crowded with bare-chested men with fake beards, wearing coarse brown breeches shredded to look like fur, and soft black shoes.

"The sadders, sir," Tom murmured. "We have to keep them apart from the nimps as long as possible. Otherwise there is high jinks, if you take my meaning."

Lord York nodded.

"I understand."

The satyrs seemed more interested in lunch than lechery at the moment. Shoving and jostling, they formed a queue leading to a table at the end of the corridor, piled high with meat pies and other fare that could be eaten easily without plates or forks.

"We find it best to provide a feed," Tom explained. "The men are apt to drink too much when they go to the taverns, and then they are good for nothing. And the women are not to be trusted outside the theater. So we keep them in."

"A wise plan," Lord York said. A lifetime of theatergoing and music-loving had taught him nothing of this. But he supposed it was well that he learned every aspect of the business, since he planned to invest in shares of the theater's royal patent, just as Tom had said.

If the opening production was a hit with London's notoriously hard-to-please audiences—and that would depend on everyone from the star of the show to the bit players now grumbling over who had snagged the largest of the meat pies—Lord York might well double or triple his investment overnight. Or he might lose it all.

They came to a nondescript door that swung open at Tom's touch. He poked his head in. "Mr. Shy? Here is Lord York."

"Thank you, Tom." Terence Shy set aside a heavy ledger that he had been poring over and stood up to greet his visitor. "Daniel—it is good of you to come. Has Tom given you the backstage tour?"

"He has. Most interesting."

Terence laughed. "I suppose you met some of the talent."

"That Molly tried her wicked wiles on him, Mr. Shy," Tom said. "I sent her packing."

"She is the boldest of the lot," Terence said. "But I am sure Daniel can look out for himself. Besides, Molly claims to be madly in love with one of the satyrs, the blond lad with the bulging calves. What is his name, Tom?"

The stage manager thought for a moment. "Oh, you mean Charlie. No, that was last week. She has throwed him over for Fred."

"The furry little fellow? You don't say." Terence seemed mightily amused. "We didn't have to issue him a beard, Daniel. Fred grew his own and a luxuriant specimen it is."

"He has a powerful roar as well for so small a man," Tom added. "Deep and loud enough to be heard over the whole damned audience on opening night."

"Yes, they never stop chattering, do they? There seems to be nothing anyone can do about it."

Lord York raised an eyebrow. "I understood that you intended to raise the tone of this theater, Terence, and attract a more elegant clientele."

Terence shrugged. "The *ton* comes to the theater to see and be seen. I dare not dim the houselights for that reason. If Lord Rake wishes to admire Lady Fickle's bountiful décolletage and whisper sweet nothings in her ear while her husband is looking the other way, who am I to stop them? Especially if they are all subscribers."

"Still, the upper classes ought to prefer intelligent entertainment."

Terence shook his head. "They enjoy low humor just as much as the rabble in the pit."

"Perhaps if the gin sellers were discouraged, the crowd would be more decorous."

Tom held up a hand. "It is not the gin sellers' fault. Me old mother, bless her sainted memory, sold gin. More money innit than oranges, she always said. She started out as an orange-girl at the Drury Lane Theater before she came here to Covent Garden."

"Nell Gwynn followed a similar path, as I recall," Terence mused. "King Charles thought the world of her."

"So the story goes, Mr. Shy," Tom said. "Though I think me dad was an ordinary man and not royal. But Mother didn't believe in explanations. I never knew him."

A brief silence fell.

"Well, it is our good fortune that you grew up in Covent Garden," Terence said affably. "You will find, Daniel, that no one knows this theater as well as

Tom Higgins. He is an invaluable resource. Ask him anything. And he knows everybody."

"I will keep that in mind," Lord York replied.

"Now then, we have much to discuss. Tom, ask Ginny Goodchurch to bring us a bottle of port, and see if you can nab four or five meat pies before the satyrs devour them all. I find that I am dreadfully hungry."

Tom looked doubtful. "They will complain, Mr. Shy. If we can't pay the actors, we must feed them."

"Take only two pies then," Terence said irritably. "The satyrs won't bite."

"You never know, sir," Tom said. "Some of 'em seems quite ferocious."

Terence gave him an exasperated look. "They have intimidated you, that is clear."

"No, but I sympathize wif 'em. I have not been paid meself."

"You will be," Tom said. "As we all know, there are only two legitimate theaters in London. Our performers—and you, Tom—have nowhere else to go, unless you want to play the provinces."

Tom shuddered.

"Remind everyone that Lizzie Loudermilk is sure to sell out the house. She always does. Just you wait."

"How long?" Tom said with a stubborn frown.

"Until the box office receipts are tallied on opening night. We will be sitting atop a mountain of golden guineas, my good man."

Terence's breezy assurances made Lord York uneasy. But he said nothing. Fortunes had been made in the theater, and it was his task to listen and learn. He reminded himself that fortunes had also been lost and to listen very carefully.

"Beggin' yer pardon, sir, but opening night is weeks away."

"What of it?" Terence said airily.

Lord York did not approve of rob-Peter-to-pay-Paul financial management. He wondered what he was getting into. Still, what choice did he have? The ever-increasing debts on his family's vast holdings would not go away. Borrowing more money was out of the question. There were mortgages too numerous to count as it was.

Gerald, his older brother, who had come into the title and was now the earl, paid not the slightest attention to such matters. In fact, Gerald was gambling away their inheritance at a terrifying rate. They might lose everything on the next roll of the dice.

It had fallen to Daniel, the dutiful second son, to step in. According to his solicitors and his banker, a gray-whiskered gentleman of grave mien, the entire estate was at risk: the country house in Richmond and the Mayfair house in London, the acres of farmland worked by generations of their tenants, the deer park and the carefully tended gardens of botanical rarities—everything Lord York held dear.

He had liquidated assets left to him by his late mama to buy shares in this theater, though his inborn prudence made him reserve more than half of his cash. When it came right down to it, he was buying shares of Lizzie Loudermilk. *If* the famous singer drew the crowds that Terence expected—*if* the production ran for months and recouped its costs—*if* he could make the next round of payments on the estate debts . . . He did not even want to count the number of *ifs*.

Chapter Two

An hour or so later, a young woman dressed in a pale blue gown and white silk slippers paused in front of an office door.

Josephine Shy could just make out the low buzz of masculine conversation and recognized the voices of her older brother, Terence, and the visitor he had been expecting, Lord Daniel York, a childhood friend. Precisely what they were saying was not clear. She listened more closely, her ear to the door.

Aha. They were discussing an immense frog they had never managed to catch and laughing immoderately. She remembered that frog.

Terence and Daniel were big boys of thirteen then, and Jo, just four. Her nursemaid had allowed her to sit on the riverbank and watch the young hunters pursue the frog, which always eluded their grasp with a thrilling leap.

Daniel had been kind to her, in an absentminded, big-brotherly way. He had even invited her family to the great house for impromptu musicales when Jo was a little older, much taken by her singing voice, which he compared to a nightingale's, and joining in with his own unsteady baritone.

By the sound of it, his voice had improved and become much deeper and deliciously mellow. But Jo was well aware that she ought not to be listening at doors, and she felt a little guilty.

She had hoped that their meeting would prove happy. It seemed to be at an end.

She heard Lord York push back his chair and begin his good-byes, mentioning urgent business in the City and an afternoon meeting with his solicitors. He promised to call on Terence again and very soon.

Josephine continued down the corridor, smiling to herself. How well did Lord York remember her? Perhaps not at all. Why would he? She had been a plain child and quiet, a vicar's daughter. He was the scion of a wealthy and powerful family, and had much more important things to think about than a little girl he had once known, the sister of a boyhood friend.

Her brilliant brother, Terence, had been the one who people remarked on, his bright future seemingly assured when he left the sleepy village of Richmond for London five years ago. He had made friends with ease among the wealthy and well-connected, but Terence's early promise had come to naught.

Yet Lord York had remained loyal, she knew.

Josephine had been delighted to see him again, though she had made sure Lord York did not see her. She had followed him through the backstage corridors, observing his embarrassing encounter with Molly; and watched from behind the stage curtain, muffling her laughter when he *baaed* at Signor Arlecchino.

She halted at an intersecting corridor and followed an arrowed sign that pointed to the dressing rooms. There was no one about. She broke into song, as she liked to do when she was alone.

Jo walked with confidence, having quickly learned her way through the many corridors and staircases that honeycombed the back of the huge theater. The dressing rooms were some distance away.

Even Terence, who had taken over the theater's management months before her arrival, was not as familiar with the building, relying on Tom Higgins and her to be his eyes and ears. He seemed happy that she was at home there; but he thought it best not to tell their parents or anyone else that Josephine spent so much of her time at the theater. She assumed that Terence wished to seem as respectable as possible and at least *appear* to observe the necessary proprieties.

Her father, now retired, and her mother, whose health was frail, would have been shocked to know the truth: Josephine, like her brother, adored the theater.

He had gone into it as a moneymaking venture, acquiring the right to run Covent Garden and its company of players on little more than a whim. Her brother had not done as well in life as he had expected, and had not found an heiress who would have him.

But she wondered at times if the responsibility was all too much for him. In desperation, Terence had written to her a few months ago and begged her to come to London. She had said yes at once, thinking it would be a lark.

Josephine supposed she would have to go back to Richmond eventually but could not imagine doing so. She hoped to remain in London forever.

It was a pleasant fantasy and unlikely to ever come true.

But, thanks to Terence's imaginative correspondence, which made up in verbiage what it lacked in truthfulness, their parents assumed that she was living quietly in the house he rented on Guilford Street, near Queen Square. They had also been told that their son was interviewing prospective suitors by the score, that he permitted his sister to attend only the most sedate balls and afternoon assemblies, and that she was always in bed by nine.

It seemed a great pity to disillusion them.

But Josephine had no desire to live as she had in Richmond. In truth, she had been in danger of perishing from boredom before she came to London. She had answered her brother's summons with joy, knowing that she could not endure one more twittering tea party with the other unmarried young women in her social circle, or devote another evening to the dreary art of cross-stitchery.

Her life in London was free of such constraints, and Terence let her do as she pleased. In fact, she worried about him more than he worried about her.

Her brother had become moody, given to maniacal bursts of energy that alternated with fits of gloom. She had no idea why, or what she might do to alleviate his mental misery. Perhaps he suffered from the strain of trying to do a hundred things at once.

That was something else she did not wish to explain to their parents. Her dear brother might yet succeed. He was certainly trying.

Terence had told her that he had asked Lord York to invest in the theater and buy shares in the royal patent he himself had bought with borrowed money. The scheme was complex but perfectly legal. Nonetheless, Josephine did not understand how her brother could ever pay back what he already owed.

Having to pay Lizzie Loudermilk's outrageous salary in full and in advance had not helped matters. The star proved to be well able to negotiate a lucrative contract for herself, saying that she was no one's fool. She'd sung for her supper as a young girl and no one got the better of Lizzie Loudermilk.

Many of the lesser performers had been lured by the prospect of appearing on the same stage with Lizzie, hoping that her fame would rub off on them. They had not yet received their wages, Josephine knew. A throng of creditors was also awaiting payment. Fending them off with carefully phrased letters and endless promises was Jo's job. And it was not the only one.

She was also Lizzie's understudy. Josephine had agreed to it only because no one had ever replaced the singer onstage. She never got sick. Jo's reputation was safe enough.

Jo turned the corner of the long corridor and headed down another one, tracing her fingertips along the rough brick wall, thinking.

Lizzie was as famous for her robust constitution as she was for the beauty and remarkable power of her voice. She had listened to Jo sing, of course— she would not have accepted her as an understudy otherwise—and seemed much impressed by the purity of the younger woman's soprano. But Lizzie had made it quite clear that she never, ever missed a performance and that Jo was not to get her hopes up.

Jo did not care in the least. She loved to sing but she had no ambition to perform, and treading the boards was quite out of the question for a vicar's daughter, anyway.

She finally arrived at the door to Lizzie's dressing room and knocked. "Miss Loudermilk?" she called. "May I come in?"

Chapter Three

"Enter!" Lizzie trilled.

Josephine opened the door and looked around it to see the singer standing in front of a tall mirror. Lizzie was clutching an unfastened corset to her magnificent bosom. Other than that, she wore only drawers and seemed not to care who saw what.

Jo looked away. A blithe disregard for propriety was simply a part of life in the theater, but Jo was not yet used to such brazenness.

"Hallo, Josie," the singer said cheerfully. "You are about to witness a miracle."

Dora, Lizzie's dresser, wrapped the corset laces around her hands and seemed to say a silent prayer. Then she pulled with all her might, stopping only to wipe the sweat from her brow.

"Oof!" Lizzie exclaimed. "Can't breathe, let alone sing!"

Dora loosened the laces just a little.

"Thank you." Lizzie let out a few experimental tra-la-las and a lace snapped. "No, this one won't do. Four strong men could not fasten my stays." She slapped her thick middle and gave her reflection a satisfied smile. "I like to eat."

Her dresser scowled and unwound the broken lace from one hand, letting the other dangle from the back of the corset.

"Don't look so cross, Dora. I don't care. Find a bigger corset or two in the wardrobe room and bring them back quick, before I get any plumper. And bring back four strong men while you're at it. Much obliged!" Lizzie let out a bawdy laugh.

Dora managed a small smile. "Yes, Miss Loudermilk."

Waiting to one side was the wardrobe mistress, Ginny Goodchurch, who also served in an unofficial capacity as mother hen of the company. Her arms were full of costumes and a pincushion was strapped to one wrist. A wicked-looking pair of shears hung from a cord around her neck.

"Jo, dear," Ginny said, "we was in the middle of a fitting, as ye can see. Can ye help?"

"Of course."

"Get one that is two sizes larger. Or three," Lizzie instructed Dora, wriggling out of the corset and handing it to her. "Dear Lord, I am ever so tired of squeezing myself into things. This show shall be the end of my brilliant career. I can't wait."

"Do not say that, Miss Loudermilk," Dora said, looking shocked. "The public will never let ye retire."

"Damn the public. I have grown weary of caterwauling for a living. And I have saved enough to retire in solitary splendor."

"But what about the old general? He has been yer devoted admirer for all these years. He will want to marry ye."

Lizzie sniffed. "I doubt it. And I do not want to marry him."

"Think of all the roses and diamonds he has given ye," Dora murmured. "And didn't he write the poem about the heavenly stars that twinkle in yer eyes?"

"No. You must be thinking of the old admiral. He was always writing poetry when he should have been off fighting the filthy French. Military men are not what they used to be, though I will always love a uniform."

"Still, it were a lovely poem," Dora said stubbornly. "You kept it in yer album for the longest time."

"Did I?" Lizzie shrugged. "It meant nothing to me."

The dresser heaved a sigh and left the room with the corset.

"She is an incurable romantic. But I am not." Lizzie studied herself in the mirror, pulling up the loose skin under her chin and frowning. "I am getting old myself. But I have no wish to listen to the general grumble about his gouty toe and the ill wind that blows through his guts. I would rather amuse myself alone or enjoy the company of dear friends—and I have many."

Ginny laughed. "And I count meself among them. But I am not sure young Jo should hear such cynical talk."

"It is the truth, Ginny. Besides, Jo has a beautiful voice that may well prove to be her fortune. What woman would marry if she could earn a handsome living on her own?" Lizzie favored Jo with a shrewd smile and returned to the contemplation of her reflection.

Josephine gaped at Lizzie's back, startled beyond words by the unexpected compliment. As to the rest of it, Lizzie had a point.

But . . . there was no escaping the social rules and conventions that shaped women's lives, however much Jo might relish her freedom at the moment and however tempting independence might seem. She would never go on the stage. No decent woman did.

"What d'ye think, Jo?" the wardrobe mistress asked. "D'ye hope to marry? I expect ye have a sweetheart."

"Ah, I do not. As for marrying, I could not say. But it is certainly very kind of Miss Loudermilk to praise my singing."

Lizzie guffawed. "Don't be mealy-mouthed, my girl. If you want all of London at your feet, you have what it takes. I know a fine voice when I hear one. But do not step into my spotlight. Not yet."

Ginny held out the costumes. "I'm sure our Jo has more sense than that. Now choose, Lizzie dear. I haven't got all day."

"Is it day? Or night? I can never tell when I'm working, and there are no windows in these stuffy little dressing rooms. We never get a breath of fresh air. Never see the sky. Never hear a sparrow sing. Strike up the violins, someone."

"Ye're a proper sketch, Lizzie," the wardrobe mistress said fondly.

Lizzie grinned and poked through the brightly colored heap of dresses in Ginny's arms. She selected a striped gown. "This one. The stripes will make me look a stone or two lighter."

"I thought ye didn't care," Ginny teased.

"Shut up or I'll have you sacked. The color is flattering. Can you let out the seams?"

Ginny set the others down and held the striped gown up to Lizzie's big body. "There might be enough material, ye great cow." She glanced over as the door opened and the dresser entered. "Here is Dora. Jo and I will pick out the seams while ye try on more corsets. Good luck."

Josephine and Ginny turned the gown inside out and spread it between them on the sofa. They concentrated on the painstaking task of unpicking the seams, and soon had the back and front of the gown apart.

Ginny examined the pieces carefully. "More than enough—there is at least an extra two inches."

"Good," Lizzie said, winking at the wardrobe mistress. "Make the most of it."

Ginny turned to Jo. "Watch how I do it so ye can learn. But it will be faster if I do the sewing meself."

Josephine knew that the wardrobe mistress was being tactful. She had tried once before to help Ginny sew, but as with her embroidery at home, the thread tangled and the needle slipped from her fingers, until she gave up in disgust.

Ginny looked for matching thread, but there was none in her basket. She set aside the pieces of the gown and walked to the door.

"Where are you off to?" Lizzie asked, tucking her overflowing bosom into the corset Dora had just put around her. Her breasts popped back up. "Blast. We need the biggest one, I'm afraid."

"Well, I need thread."

Lizzie nodded regally. "You may go."

Ginny rolled her eyes for Jo's benefit and left the room. Lizzie and Dora wrestled with another set of stays, talking in low voices, while Jo leaned back on the squeaky old sofa and looked around the dressing room.

Like all theater folk, Lizzie Loudermilk was superstitious—and messy. The dressing table, folding screen, and walls were decorated with trinkets that were supposed to bring luck. Imitation pearl necklaces and sham jewels dangled from the candleholders on either side of the dressing table mirror. Letters from admirers and invitations to dances and dinners were tucked into its frame.

A faded garter had pride of place at the mirror's top. Ginny had explained that Lizzie had worn it for her triumphant debut at Covent Garden years ago, when Ginny and the singer had met for the first time.

Josephine tried to imagine singing while looking out on a crowd of more than three thousand people. She could never do it—not with her eyes open, anyway.

She rose and went to the dressing table, casting a glance into the hinged, multicompartmented case that sat upon it. Each compartment held something different: small brushes, sticks of charcoal, powdered pigments wrapped in crinkly paper, tiny velvet patches, strange bits of rubber, and little pots of thick paint.

Josephine picked up a brush and touched it to her palm, surprised by the softness of the bristles.

Lizzie smiled. "That's sable, love. Made especially for me. Dip it in the pink powder and give yourself nice rosy cheeks. You look a bit pale."

Josephine hastily set down the brush. "I would never."

"What are you afraid of?"

My mother, Jo wanted to say. *My father. Everyone in Richmond.* She reminded herself that she was in London. If she wanted to look like a rosy-cheeked milkmaid—or an Indian queen or a wicked witch—they would never know. She picked up the brush again.

"Go ahead, you little goose. Have a bit of fun."

Dora gave Josephine an encouraging smile. "Yes,

do. It is only paint and powder, miss." She pointed to a fat jar in front of the mirror. "That there is a cream to take it all off again."

Jo sat down in front of the mirror and stared at her reflection. She saw what she always saw: regular features, pale skin with a few freckles, a curving mouth with a full lower lip. Her eyes were a mix of blue and green, with long lashes. Her hair was the color of honey and she wore it up, with a fringe.

She looked no different than yesterday but she suddenly felt different. Bolder. Naughtier. Ready for a change.

"Very well, I will."

She opened a packet of pink powder and dipped the brush into it, then dabbed the powder on her cheeks. But the color was too bright against her skin and the circles were too even.

"I look like a clown," she said with dismay.

"Try again. Takes practice," Lizzie said.

Josephine picked up a rag and tried to wipe away the powder, to no avail.

"Ye have to use the cream," Dora reminded her. "But ye can put on a color over the powder if you like. Try this one." She selected a pot of skin-colored paint and opened it, setting it down in front of Jo, who wrinkled her nose.

"It smells bad."

"You get used to it," Lizzie said philosophically.

Josephine gave her a doubtful look. She wasn't at all sure that she wanted to. "But how do I put it on?"

"With yer fingertips. 'Tis greasy, miss. So ye can't use the sable brush. And ye won't want to get it in yer hair. Here, let me." Dora picked up a piece of fine gauze and wound it tightly around Jo's head, tucking every last strand of hair underneath.

Jo peered in the mirror again. "Oh, dear. Now I look like a bald clown."

Dora laughed. "D'ye want me to show ye how to put on a face?"

"Yes, please do. I shall never manage on my own."

With Lizzie on one side making suggestions and Dora on the other doing the work, Jo watched in the mirror as an amazing transformation took place. Her plain self gradually disappeared . . . and a bewitching creature with arched eyebrows, ruby lips, and a china-doll complexion took her place. When Dora removed the gauze to redo Josephine's hair, she scarcely recognized herself.

Dora pinned up Jo's hair anew, and Lizzie added a collar of imitation pearls and paste earbobs. In the candlelight, they looked real enough, and Josephine looked spectacular.

"You are a beauty, miss," Dora said admiringly.

Lizzie nodded. "I must agree."

"It is only the paint," Jo said hastily. "That's not me."

"It is you," Lizzie replied. "Do you know, looking at you makes me feel tired. Very tired. And very old."

"You are not old, Miss Loudermilk," Dora said quietly.

"At the moment, I feel older than Mrs. Methuselah. Unless Methuselah was married to a younger woman—I'm sure he was. All the old goats want a young woman. That is a fact of life, Josephine. Make a note of it."

Jo didn't know whether to laugh or say something sympathetic. She had intended only to amuse herself, not to show up Lizzie.

But Jo had not expected to look so . . . dazzling.

She had never looked dazzling before. It was an interesting sensation. She peered into the mirror again to see whether the beautiful lady had gone away. No, there she was.

"Look your fill," Lizzie said gloomily. "Enjoy it while it lasts and gather ye rosebuds while ye may, et cetera. Perhaps I should have a lie-down." She got up with a dejected sigh and went over to the sofa, pulling a tattered old blanket up over her face. "It is later than I think."

Jo looked worriedly at Dora and then back in the mirror. She knew that it was a face for the footlights and not in the least real, but her transformation had certainly alarmed Lizzie. Jo wondered whether to reassure the singer.

"Never mind her, miss. She'll stop sulking soon enough," Dora said rather loudly.

"I am not sulking," the old blanket replied with muffled dignity. "I am resting. And planning my retirement from the stage. I mean it this time. This show will definitely mark my final appearance upon the boards."

"Ye keep sayin' that, Miss Loudermilk. And I keep tellin' ye, the public will not let ye retire."

A knock on the door made Lizzie fling off the blanket and sit up. Her riotous red hair curled in every direction and spilled over her shoulders. The two women at the dressing table turned around.

"Now who do ye suppose that is?" Dora asked.

"Ask," Lizzie hissed. "Ginny would not knock."

There was another knock. "Hello? Is Miss Loudermilk within?"

"Yes, kind sir, I sit and spin," she sang under her breath.

"One of your greatest admirers would like to meet you."

Jo recognized her brother's voice. "It is Terence . . .

and he would not like to see me painted and powdered."

"Then get in the closet," Lizzie said, rolling her
eyes. "Always a good beginning for a farce."

Josephine took a deep breath. At least Lord
York had left the theater. She would be dreadfully
embarrassed if he saw her like this. Even if her
brother was accompanied by a stranger, she would
still be embarrassed. She decided that she might as
well hide.

"One moment," Lizzie called. She got up and
threw on a threadbare robe of greenish-gray material, inspecting herself in the tall mirror. "Dear God,
it *is* later than I think. I look dead." She whipped
off the robe, found another in a flattering peach
color and put it on instead. "Are you with the admiral or the general?" she called to the door.

"Neither," Terence said from the other side.

"What do I care?" Lizzie muttered. "I need an
admirer at the moment. Any bloke will do." She
cast a look at Josephine. "Quick! Into the closet!"

Chapter Four

From inside the closet, Jo heard her brother enter. She clutched the doors from the inside—they had not latched.

"Only two of you?" he said, nodding to Dora. "I thought I heard three voices."

Lizzie made a great fuss over tying the sash of her robe and tossed her hair. "No, just us." She cast an appraising glance at Lord York.

"Miss Loudermilk, allow me to introduce Lord York."

"How do you do."

Drat and double drat, Jo thought. Lord York had not gone after all.

Her nose twitched. She could not sneeze. The thick, greasy makeup began to itch. She could not let go of the doors to scratch. She fervently hoped and prayed that their visitors would pay Lizzie the extravagant compliments that the singer craved, and leave at once.

She heard someone settle onto the squeaky old sofa, and then a faint thump. This she recognized as the sound of good leather boots crossing at the

ankle. Damnation. Did Terence have nothing better to do than loiter in dressing rooms?

"Hello, Ginny," he said.

"Hello, Mr. Shy." The wardrobe mistress came in
and spoke to Lizzie. "I cannot find the exact color.
I will have to go out and buy more thread. Or I
might send Jo. Where is she?"

Josephine winced.

"Yes, where is my sister?" Terence asked. "We
thought we might find her here. The dancers told
me they saw her head off this way."

"Did they?" said Lizzie. "Oh, um, she was here
but she went out to . . . to the apothecary. For
medicated gargle. For my throat. She is a dear and
always so thoughtful."

"Ah, yes," Lord York said. "She is a dear. How
does Jo like London, Terence? And does she still
sing? I remember her warbling in the lanes of
Richmond."

You do? Jo opened her mouth in surprise, then
shut it quickly.

"She had a lovely voice, even when she was very
young," Lord York went on. "Do you recollect that
musical evening at Derrydale, when she and I sang
a duet?"

"Vaguely," Terence said.

"You and I were seventeen."

"And she was a brat of eight." Terence laughed.

"Then you and I remember her differently. She
was charming, even as a child. I seldom saw her
after that, and then only at a distance, but she did
seem to have grown into a lovely young woman."

Thank you very much, Jo thought crossly, rubbing
her itchy nose against the door. *You might have told
me.* No doubt Lord York thought himself too grand
for a mere vicar's daughter.

"Has she married?" he asked.

"No."

Why did he want to know?

"You never did say if she likes London, Terence."

"She seems to like it well enough. She is a busy little bee and quite domestic—she keeps house for me, you know."

Liar.

"And she never comes to the theater," Terence said firmly. "Well, almost never."

"I should think she would be tempted to sing upon that marvelous stage, if only to an empty house."

"Jo? Not at all. No decent woman would even think of such a thing."

"But if no one was listening and no one knew, Terence, what would it matter?"

The two men pondered that conundrum for a moment.

Lizzie, who hated to be ignored, stamped a foot. "Am I not a decent woman? And what is wrong with singing in a theater? There are worse ways to make money. At least theater folk are honest—and virtuous when it counts."

Terence laughed nervously. "That is a cynical thing to say."

"Do you know," Lizzie said, putting her hands on her hips and assuming a belligerent stance, "that is the second time today someone has told me that. I must not be as innocent as I once was. Sad, isn't it? Getting old is hell."

"My dear Miss Loudermilk," Terence began, "you are ageless. The public loves you. Your very name is enough to make them line up at the box office and buy tickets by the score."

Lizzie sniffed, only somewhat mollified. "I suppose so."

Inside the closet, crammed as it was with gowns

and other garments, Jo felt more and more as if she might suffocate. A wig tumbled from the top shelf but she caught it in time, now holding the doors closed with one hand.

The wig had been heavily powdered. The tickling inside her nose was nearly unbearable. She was going to sneeze. She could not help it.

"Miss Loudermilk, it is a very great pleasure to meet you in person," Lord York said. "I have attended many of your London concerts over the years, of course."

Josephine could almost hear the singer smile. "Did you see me in Paris last year?"

"The *Swan Song* opera? Yes, I did. But I am glad that it was not your last farewell, as advertised."

"Well, no. More like the next-to-last-semifinal farewell. It is hard to say good-bye when the crowds scream for more." She preened a bit and Dora sighed.

"Ye cannot retire now. Ye'd be ever so bored, Miss Loudermilk."

"I could write my memoirs," the singer said.

"No doubt there will be a run on the booksellers if you do," Terence said. "Those who are mentioned will be outraged and those who are left out will be relieved. Either way, your honesty will ensure that the book flies off the shelves."

"Quite," Lizzie said smugly. "And now, gentlemen, I must prime the pipes."

Lord York raised a quizzical eyebrow.

"I am referring to my vocal exercises. La-la-la and lo-lo-lo. Hee-hee-hee and ha-ha-ha."

Dora, mindful of the prisoner in the closet, jumped up to show the men out. "She can break glass on the high notes. It is most impressive."

Terence patted his waistcoat pocket. "My spectacles are safely tucked away. Come, Daniel, let us leave these dear ladies and look for my sister. I am sure she is not far away."

"Good-bye," said Lizzie. "Do come again."

Dora did the honors and then shut the door, propping a chair under the knob.

Lizzie strode to the closet and Josephine stumbled out, gasping for air and waving the wig. "Oh, the dust—I was just about to sneeze!"

Dora took the wig and stuffed it back on the top shelf. "Ye poor thing. They are gone, as ye can see. Sit down and I will help ye get all that muck off yer face."

"Thank you, Dora."

Jo's eyes were watering. She let the dresser steer her to the table and apply the soothing cream.

"Lord York seems to admire you, Jo," Lizzie said, looking absentmindedly at her music. "La-la-la. Lo-lo-lo."

"I can't imagine why," Josephine replied. She let her eyelids drift shut as Dora removed the makeup with gentle strokes. When she opened her eyes, she was just plain Jo again. She rather missed the painted hussy in the mirror.

Lord Daniel entered the great and gloomy house in Mayfair, nodding to the butler who opened the door and took his hat and gloves.

His heels clicked on the cold marble floor, a sound that echoed up the stairwell. There was no one at home but the newly hired servants, whose names he did not know. They came and went like specters, rarely speaking. The house was immaculate; meals were served punctually and perfectly; and everything he needed appeared as if by magic, without his even having to ask.

He hated it.

His brother had sacked the family retainers en masse upon coming into the title and hired this lot to replace them. Where Gerald had found such quiet, ghostly ones was a mystery. Perhaps at an undertaker's, Daniel thought, feeling rather depressed.

But he could not ask Gerald, who was traveling— or perhaps carousing would be a better word— somewhere on the Continent and would not return for months. Daniel had the Mayfair house to himself . . . not that he wanted to be alone.

The Covent Garden Theater, from which he had just returned, was a much more inviting place. The camaraderie and coarse jokes of the idle performers had cheered him, as had the stage manager's open friendliness. Seeing Terence again and talking over old times had been a tonic.

His mercurial friend seemed well suited to the theater and its myriad, ever-changing demands, if not the accounting part of it. Daniel knew he would have to go over the books to protect his investment. He had been blessed—or should he say cursed?— with a sense of responsibility in such matters.

He moved through the front hall, his wayward thoughts settling on Terence's sister. So she was in London now, and keeping house for him. Interesting.

He wished that he had gone more often to the Richmond cottage. He had thought of it each time he happened to see Jo in the lanes. He had known at the time, vaguely, that she had turned sixteen, seventeen, eighteen . . . and then, somehow, twenty-one, still living with her parents. But he had been preoccupied with family matters during his father's long last illness and set aside his fond thoughts of

Josephine Shy. His chance meeting with Terence a few months ago had brought back memories that were poignant for all that they were few.

He had last seen her in Richmond, shopping on the main street with her mother, but she had not seen him. Had he not been in a closed carriage, rushing to London to transact some estate business, he would have stopped to talk to her then.

A basket over her arm, a bonnet tied under her pretty chin, her shapely form in clinging muslin— she was the very picture of a lovely village girl, a true English rose, just budded. And he knew she would grow in beauty as the years passed. Jo had never been conventionally pretty, but he found her irresistibly attractive nonetheless. And those few times—alas, from a distance—when he had heard her sing, as freely and naturally as a bird, were not something he would ever forget.

The women of the *ton* did not compare to Jo. The ones he had met and been introduced to by well-meaning friends seemed to resemble their little dogs more often than not, carefully groomed and snappish.

He could not imagine that Jo would find friends among them. But what else did she do? Keeping house for her brother hardly seemed like something she would enjoy, but Terence had said that she liked nothing better.

Daniel went into the library, where a fire burned brightly behind the grate. It was the only touch of life in the whole damned house.

He allowed himself to slump in an armchair, studying the flickering display of red and gold . . . and thinking far into the night.

Chapter Five

Two weeks later...

Incessant rain had brought rehearsals to a halt.
The roof was leaking and there were puddles on
the stage. Josephine had tired of helping Lizzie
practice her scales, and wandered about in a black
mood.

All of the Covent Garden players were on edge
and quarrelsome, unable to practice their steps or
block out scenes or invent bits of stage business to
amuse the audience who would see them on opening night.

Some of the dancers had taken up residence in
the boxes of the upper galleries, under strict instructions from Tom Higgins not to do any dam-
age. Jo could see their heads and hear their faint
chatter.

They were undoubtedly gossiping and telling
bawdy stories of stage-door Romeos while they attended to the routine chores of mending stockings and shoes.

Jo looked out upon the rows of benches that stretched far back beyond the pit, and noticed a performer napping on one here and there. The theater was cold and drafty, and its echoing loneliness was disagreeable in the extreme.

Jo went through the door in the proscenium arch and headed for her brother's office, wanting to see how he was faring on this dreary day.

"There you are, Terence. What are you doing?"

He gave her a wild-eyed look and slammed the ledger he had been poring over shut. "Tearing out my hair!"

"Why?"

"That is an easy question to answer. The books do not balance. The entries do not add up. I am at my wit's end!" He pushed the ledger off his desk with a sweep of his arm, and it landed atop some others on the floor. "I suspect that the previous owner was skimming the receipts. He paid no one but himself. I must make good on his debts and ours, if the show is to go on."

"Is it that bad?"

"The prop master tells me that he is nearly out of materials and not all the sets are built. We shall have to improvise, he says."

"It will all come round right in the end, I am sure," Jo said soothingly.

"I am not," Terence replied. "Have you written to our creditors?"

"Yes. Again. All of them."

"Then there is nothing more I can do. I am counting on Lizzie, but I must confess, knowing that so much depends on one person's performance alarms me."

"She will be a howling success," Jo said.

"Dear me. Where did you pick up that expression?"

"Lizzie, of course. She is an original in every way. As she likes to say, there is only one Lizzie Loudermilk."

"Thank God for that. She has been extraordinarily irritable lately. She does seem to like you, though, and I am grateful for that."

"I have learned much about singing from her, Terence. How to project the voice, for one, and how to breathe properly so as not to strain it."

Terence shrugged. "Yes, well, it is good advice, but you will not have an opportunity to put it into practice. I cannot let you perform, my dear Jo."

"I don't want to," she said simply.

Terence studied his sister for a long moment. "What *do* you want to do? I suppose I have been remiss in my brotherly obligations. I should have found you a suitable fiancé by now: a worthy fellow, with a comfortable income and no major vices. You could be quite cozy, embroidering his monogram on every little thing, as wives do."

Josephine made a face.

"Forgive me. I forgot how much you hate sewing."

"Ginny won't let me, you know. Oh, I do need something to do."

Terence got up to pace upon the carpet, his hands clasped behind his back. "We have added a singing castaway and he requires a desert island. You could help the prop master."

"A castaway? Why?"

"Read the *Spectator*. True stories are all the rage on stage. Hugh Newsome seemed inspired by this one. Fortunately, it does not require an erupting volcano or a naval battle."

"We do have a ship backdrop, Terence."

He smiled at his sister. "You seem to know more than I about this theater."

She smiled back. "Perhaps."

Terence found the newspaper on the floor and gave it to her. "A Nantucket whaling ship found a poor fellow who had been cast away for ten years in the middle of the Pacific. If you are bored, imagine how he felt."

Josephine found the article and read it quickly. "He seems happy to be in London."

"Of course. He is the toast of the town, now that he has shaved off his fearsome beard. And I have heard that he never sleeps alone. But that is to be expected after a decade of deprivation."

"The *Spectator* doesn't mention that, Terence," she said, laughing.

"No. And they don't seem to know, either, that the unfortunate man was rescued by a giant white bird and not Yankee sailors."

"What?"

"Hugh thought a giant bird would add something to the castaway scene. He said it was a symbol of something. Damned if I can remember what."

"Who will play the bird?"

"Molly. She has no fear of swinging on a wire or of heights." He stopped his pacing and struck a dramatic pose. "The curtain will rise on a group of barren rocks. A lean and weather-beaten man with barnacles in his beard appears. The castaway crawls over the jagged rocks, singing merrily—"

"Surely he is not merry."

"No, of course not. I am making fun of Hugh's pretensions. He hopes to write a tragedy of epic stature."

"Oh, no."

"I can't stop him if I can't pay him," Terence said.

"Well, what does the castaway sing about?"

"Sing a song of sunburn," her brother improvised, *"baked under the sky.* I don't know. Hugh is still writing the lyrics. And McNeel is working on the rocks today."

Jo nodded. "Then I shall help him. Mama taught me to paint scenery upon plates."

"A ladylike art that has ruined a great deal of perfectly good china," Terence said. "Well, then you are a dab hand with a brush and now you have something to do. I must return to my work. Daniel is coming by shortly. He wishes to examine the books."

Jo wondered what Lord York would think if he knew that she was the one who kept their creditors at bay. Certainly it was no more respectable than singing on a stage. He would not approve. "Must I continue to avoid him?"

"Unfortunately, I made a point of saying that you almost never come to the theater. Shall I arrange a tea party at Guilford Street, and find a suitable chaperone? Are you interested in him, Jo?"

The blunt question made her gulp. "I . . . I have not spoken to him in years. But I did catch a glimpse of him during his first visit."

"Aha! He mentioned halfway through our bottle of port that he thought someone was following him. But he said he must have been imagining things. So it was you."

Jo looked archly at him. "He is a handsome man, and according to you, a good one."

"He may be too good," Terence said wryly. "But if you find him attractive, I see no need for missish simpering. I did promise Mama and Papa that I would find you a husband, and Daniel might do very well. He remembers you fondly and said as much when we visited Lizzie in her dressing room."

Really, she wanted to say. *And it was ever so nice of you to tell him I was a brat.* She was not at all sure that her eccentric brother would prove reliable as a matchmaker.

"Have you told him about the singing castaway?"

Terence shook his head. "Not yet. He will not be pleased. He wanted us to offer noble dramas on elevated subjects."

"Oh, he will enjoy the spectacle of a great white bird, like everyone else."

"I hope so. Any excuse to have a performer fly. The crowd will go wild even if Daniel does not."

"You are becoming an impresario, Terence. I think that the theater suits you. Despite the financial difficulties, you seem to be having a wonderfully amusing time."

Terence laughed. "I am at that. It is like being mayor of a city. A very strange sort of city where day and night change places, and everything is pretense. The houses are nothing more than teetering façades and the doors open to nowhere. As for the inhabitants . . . they are entirely mad."

"But certainly entertaining."

"Yes, and perhaps I am a little mad myself." Terence ran a hand through his hair. "Now then. I am sure you have met the prop master."

"In passing. His name is McNeel, is it not?"

"It is. His workshop is in the building next door, but there is a connecting corridor."

"It must be the only one that I do not know."

"I will show you the way."

He offered his arm to her with a gentlemanly flourish, and Jo took it.

In due time, the two Shys found themselves outside a door marked with the words *McNeel's Stage Properties and Special Theatrical Effects—Keep Owt.* They opened it and went in.

Jo looked about, wrinkling her nose at the strong smell of turpentine. Terence made the necessary introductions and explanations, and left them to it.

McNeel showed her a cluster of artificial rocks, turning them this way and that in different groupings. A ladder was built into the back of the biggest one.

"So ye want to paint? Ye will need a smock, Miss Shy." He indicated a rack of baggy, paint-spattered garments.

She picked the smallest and least dirty, and slipped it on over her dress. "My brother says you are making a desert island. How exciting!"

McNeel shook his head. "I cannot get the color quite right. They lack something. Rockiness, I suppose. They are too alike."

She looked at the rocks, which were painted a uniform gray. "I think that they are very nice," she said encouragingly.

"They need detail."

The door banged and Jo turned around. Molly entered, wearing a wrapper over a nondescript dress and eating shelled nuts from a paper sack. Josephine was surprised to see a big green-and-yellow parrot perched on the dancer's shoulder.

"Will ye look at that!" said McNeel. "Molly, may we put the parrot in the castaway scene? I can make him his own wee palm tree to sit in."

"He likes me shoulder better," Molly said. She popped a nut in her mouth and gave one to the parrot. He took it with great dexterity, turning it round in his black, leathery claw before putting it in his beak and eating it.

"He is wonderful," Jo said. She had never seen a parrot up close and longed to feed him a nut herself.

"That's me Nippy," Molly said proudly. "He's a love and much less trouble than a man. Goes right to sleep when you throw a cloth over his cage. Show me a man who can do that."

Nippy let out an *awk* of agreement.

Jo reached out a hand to touch his beautiful plumage.

"Ow, Miss Shy, be careful. Nippy by name, nippy by nature."

Jo let her hand drop. His beak was impressive.

"Now then," McNeel interrupted. "Have ye tried out the wire, Molly? The lads and I rigged it this morning before the roof leaks started."

"Aye, it is ever so much fun to fly. I gave a great screech that brought everybody running as I swung to and fro. Me feet never touched the puddles."

"That roof must be fixed before opening night." McNeel sighed.

"How will yer brother find the money for that, hey?" Molly asked Jo.

The dancer was more full of herself than ever, now that she had a solo, Josephine thought. And what a solo it would be.

Molly walked away, swinging her hips. The parrot adjusted his position accordingly, stepping a little from side to side. The sight was comical and Jo suppressed a smile.

Molly stopped at the rocks and looked them over. "These are very plain. They don't look like rocks at all."

"I could send a lad down to the docks to buy coconuts and pineapples," he suggested. "Brighten things up a bit, that would."

"Naow, that won't do neither. A half-starved castaway can't be sittin' on a heap o' fresh fruit. He's a desolate, tragical figure." She popped several nuts at once into her mouth and chewed them noisily. "My love is what saves him. Not pineapples."

McNeel walked over to a small, cluttered desk and picked up several pages of foolscap. "Did Newsome change the scene again? Tom just brought these back from the copyist." He read the first page and flipped it over to the second. "Ah, ye're right, Molly. It says here that the rocks are barren." He read on with a frown.

"Is something the matter?" Josephine inquired.

"Hugh goes on. And on. The castaway is a symbol of everyman," McNeel replied. "The rocks are a symbol of his soul, which is encrusted with sin, and the rocks should be encrusted with . . . oh, no. I'll need a flock o' seagulls to get that effect."

Jo read over his shoulder. "I have an idea, Mr. McNeel."

"Have at, my girl." He threw the sheets of paper back down on the desk.

Molly laughed and walked in a circle, with Nippy huddled against her hair. The parrot made soft chuckling noises in her ear until she fed him another nut.

"Another thing, McNeel. Mr. Shy don't think I can fly and sing at the same time, and he may be right for once."

"Aye."

"He said I should concentrate on not crashing into Andy, our castaway, and not anything else. Ye may have to make that wire a little shorter."

"We will have to work that out on stage, Molly."

She shrugged and moved away, toward the other side of the barnlike room, where Signor Arlecchino was hopping about on a scaffold, painting a green backdrop for *The Shepherdess*.

But Molly stopped to talk to the sign painter first, admiring his work. The man's face turned red from her attentions. "Bloody hell, ye're ever so talented, Bert. But can ye make my name bigger?" she asked.

Bert looked over at the prop master.

"Molly," said McNeel. His tone held a warning. "Ye are not the star of the show."

She pouted. "Andy's name is bigger than mine. 'Tisn't fair."

"Can it wait a few minutes?"

"All right."

Molly leaned all over the dumbstruck sign painter while McNeel and Jo read through the script once more to make sure they had not missed anything important. They heard her whisper and giggle to Bert. But when did Molly not whisper and giggle?

Eventually they came over to look at the signboard. It had changed somewhat.

They saw Molly scurry out the back door with Nippy on her shoulder, *awk*ing wildly. Bert hung his head, looking apologetic. All three of them studied the new sign.

~ ~ ~ ~ ~

THE COVENT GARDEN THEATER

(Under New Management)

PRESENTS
MISS LIZZIE LOUDMOUTH

as

"The Shepherdess"
In the Premiere Performance Of

A ROLL IN THE HAY
by Noted Dramatist
Hughie Wughie

~ ~ ~ ~ ~

AND IF YOU ARE BORED

BY SHEEP
AND SEVENTEEN STUPID SONGS
DON'T MISS

MOLLY
as
THE BIG WHITE BIRD OF THE SOUTH SEAS

~ ~ ~ ~ ~

"I am very sorry, sir." Bert seemed a bit dazed. "I will paint it out and start over."

"See that ye do," was all McNeel said.

Jo tried not to look at poor Bert, who was no match for the likes of Molly. But she could not help laughing.

"I admire her brass," McNeel said. "Nothing scares that girl. She likes to take chances. It is part of the reason she is good on the wire."

"Is it very risky?" Jo asked. "We must take every precaution." She wondered what those might be. Perhaps her brother had gone too far.

"She learned how from a troupe of trapeze artists. And yes, we will see that she is safe. The wire is strong and she is light."

"I suppose that you know what you are doing."

"Haven't had anyone hurt yet. Now, back to these rocks. Ye said ye had an idea."

"Yes, I do."

"Very good. Work on the rocks, then, and I'll paint the waves." He pointed to two very long pieces of wood, carefully carved to resemble breaking waves. Each end had a heavy iron handle, rather like a meat spit, Jo saw, with which they could be rotated from the wings.

"Very realistic, they are, when the stagehands get 'em going. Miss Loudermilk says that just looking at artificial waves makes her seasick."

"A good thing that she is not in the scene." Jo stood at the worktable that held the paints and deliberated for a moment. She selected a large, tightly corked jar of white gouache and shook it, uncorked it, and then poured in a dollop of black and a bit of gray.

She stuck in a narrow piece of scrap wood and twirled it about but did not mix the colors completely. McNeel watched her with interest.

Jo peered into the jar and appeared to be satisfied. She walked over to the rocks and poured the streaky mixture over the smallest one. "There you have it. Guano."

McNeel applauded. "And gorgeous guano it is! Nice work, Miss Shy. Ye may do the same to the rest of the rocks. Then we will figure out a place for Andy to do—what does he do?" He consulted the foolscap sheets again and read aloud. " 'The castaway shakes his fist at the indifferent heavens.' Damn Hugh Newsome and his flights of fancy! Does he want the sky cloudy or clear? And how am I supposed to convey indifference with paint and plaster? I wish he would give clear instructions."

Josephine took the script pages and studied them. " 'A violent storm arises in the west. The castaway cringes at the sound of thunder.' "

"Oh, well, that is easy. The stagehands shake a monstrous sheet of tin until hell won't have it, and we make the stage lamps flicker behind a scrim of dark blue silk."

"Most ingenious."

McNeel grinned. "And it is great fun."

Several hours later, the rocks were nearly dry, and Andy, the castaway, had come to see them.

"I do like what you've done with the droppings. Delightfully dismal." The actor then noted with an approving smile the ladder that McNeel had built into the back of the biggest rock. "Thanks for that, McNeel. They seem a bit flimsy and I should not want to accidentally stick a foot through one."

"No," McNeel said, "ye simply scramble up the ladder and sing. Or shake yer fist. We have just finished the indifferent heavens. Over here."

He guided Andy to the huge canvas backdrop

hanging from the rafters. A dramatic stormy sky was splashed across it, done in ominous colors with thin streaks of brilliant titanium white for the lightning.

"Splendid! Molly's costume will show up beautifully against that," Andy said.

Jo, who had been working on it with Ginny Goodchurch, waved the men over. "I am having trouble with the feathers, Mr. McNeel. The glue will not dry and they keep falling off."

"Can't have that," the prop master said. "You must sew them. Remember, Molly will be flying through the air, swinging to and fro. She can't look as if she's molting. Ruins the effect."

He touched the costume, which was pinned to a dressmaker's form, and a handful of feathers fluttered to the floor. "Where is Ginny? She will know how to fix this."

"She has gone home for the day," Jo replied.

McNeel sighed. "I wish I could. But there is too much to do and too little time. How is Signor Arlecchino coming along with the rustic scenery for *The Shepherdess*?"

He turned and looked down toward the end of the workshop, in shadow now that they were working by lamplight.

"He's gone too," Jo said.

McNeel checked the nearby shelves devoted to supplies. "Blast! Used up nearly all of the paint and the last of the canvas, he has. Come let's see what he's done."

The little group walked to the other side of the room.

"That ain't an English landscape!" McNeel said, horrified. "It looks like a damned jungle. And is that a tiger?"

"No one will care," Andy said hastily.

"*I* care," said McNeel.

"Are those white creatures supposed to be dogs or bears?" Josephine asked.

"Bears, I think, very small ones," Andy said, a hand to his chin. "It is difficult to tell. They are not fierce bears, if that matters."

McNeel groaned. "That is definitely a tiger. Just look at those glowing yellow eyes. What was Arlecchino thinking?" The prop master threw up his hands in frustration. "I explained it all twice and even gave him a picture book to work from. He seemed to understand."

Jo found the book on the floor in front of the backdrop. "He got the pictures mixed up. Look, there is the tiger. And the polar bears are on the next page, though he made them smaller. He must have been wondering what *you* were thinking. But it seems that he did the best he could."

"For what it's worth." McNeel scowled.

"Are there bears or tigers or dogs in *The Shepherdess*?" Andy asked.

"Not a one," McNeel said. "We will have to start over. But the shopkeepers will not provide more supplies until the bills are paid."

"I will see what I can do," Josephine said quietly.

Chapter Six

Breakfast was served; breakfast was eaten. As was their custom before noon, Terence and Josephine hardly spoke to each other. Guilford Street was quiet enough at this hour, and the house seemed to echo with silence.

He was presently preoccupied with the *Times*. The only sound in the room was the slow turning of its pages.

She looked about the peaceful room, noting the way the sun fell upon the light blue wallpaper and how its light crept across the table. She had quite finished her repast and there was nothing else to do. In fifteen minutes, a ray of sunlight had reached the muffins. In another ten, it reached the unfinished tea in her cup.

Terence turned the pages with excruciating calm. Shattering his composure and upsetting his digestion was the last thing she wanted to do at the moment. He would be deeply unhappy to hear that the exuberant Signor Arlecchino had used up what little canvas and paint were left, especially since

Terence was worried about money as it was. Yet she had to inform him.

"My dear Terence," she began.

He looked over the top of the paper at her. "You have never addressed me as 'dear' this early in the morning. Whatever is the matter?"

"Nothing is the matter." She sighed. "I was merely feeling affectionate, brother dear."

Terence put down the paper and gave her a narrow look. "I can count, Jo. That was two dears in quick succession, separated by one heartfelt sigh. You are attempting to butter me up. But I shall not be buttered. What is troubling you?"

Jo folded her hands in her lap. "Mr. McNeel says that we are running short of supplies to build the sets and make backdrops."

Terence opened the *Times* again. "I know that."

"We cannot present a five-hour programme without sets, Terence."

"Tell McNeel to paint the flat sets on both sides, so the stagehands can turn them around as necessary. The actors will double up on roles, and if we use only half the dancers, they can step twice as fast to make up for it."

Jo wanted to smile but decided to look serious instead. "That will not work."

He shot her an irritated look and threw the newspaper to the floor. "Jo, there is nothing I can do. You know that I cannot pay our creditors. I feel dreadfully guilty that you took on the thankless task of writing to them as it is."

"But I do not owe them the money, so it was easy enough."

"I daresay it was. And all I had to do was sign the damned letters with a flourish," he said bitterly.

"I came to London to help you, Terence,"

Josephine said. "And I don't mind writing the letters. I'm rather good at it, I find."

"It is a form of fiction, I suppose."

"You might say that," Jo replied.

"Dear sir," Terence went on in a mocking tone. "Your invoice was received with joy and examined with great interest. Rest assured that I keep it under my pillow, along with a thousand others. Please accept our promise of prompt payment, which, you will note, is not included with this letter. We will send a free ticket as soon as we can pay the engraver and have tickets printed. There will be dancing nymphs in diaphanous costumes and a singing castaway, and we do hope you will enjoy the show. I remain, very truly yours, et cetera."

Josephine got up quickly, brushing a few muffin crumbs from her *robe de chambre*. "That reminds me—I quite forgot to write to the engraver. Perhaps I will stop by his workshop today."

"I wish you would not, Jo. Mama and Papa would be furious if they ever found out how much time you spend at the theater and all the work you are doing there. I appreciate your efforts from the bottom of my heart, but *they* will not."

She did not argue or agree, but picked up the newspaper he had thrown down, looking through it to the theater reviews and glancing at them quickly. "I am sure our show will surpass whatever the Drury Lane players are offering."

"My spies tell me that they are struggling with *Cupid and the Countess*."

Her eyes opened wide. "What? Why? And who are your spies? I knew nothing of this."

"I shall answer the second question first. Apparently their leading lady and man began to actually believe the ridiculous dialogue they were spouting, and the countess ran off with Cupid just last week. They are auditioning replacements today."

"Or so say your spies. They must be members of the Drury Lane company or the crew, or someone would notice them straightaway. Am I correct?"

"Yes," Terence said, rather unwillingly.

"I cannot believe that you employ such persons."

"As Shakespeare said, all's fair in love and war," he said. "The Drury Lane Players are our rivals."

She gave him a searching look. "You would not go so far as to sabotage their production in any way, would you, Terence?"

"Certainly not," he replied. "I would never do that. I have standards, you know—lower than they used to be but standards all the same."

His tone was quite sincere and she was inclined to believe him. She had never known her brother to lie, though he was apt to exaggerate.

"I hope not, Terence. And our difficulties are only temporary. Where there's a will, there's a way."

"Did Shakespeare say that?"

"I don't know," Jo replied. "The immortal Bard of Avon seems to have said just about everything worth saying. And he wrote some bang-up good plays while he was at it."

"Please do not inform Hugh Newsome of that fact."

She turned to go, having thought things through in the little while they had been talking. She had to do something about the shortfall in supplies, and it was not absolutely necessary that Terence know every detail of her plan.

"I have not seen him for several days. Has Mr. Newsome been at the theater?"

Terence scowled. "I think he roosts upside down

in the rafters at night and keeps the bats company. All writers are a little strange. But his name on the bill counts for something."

"Has he not won praise from the critics?"

Terence thought for a moment. "Yes, one or two seemed favorably disposed to his previous work. But the riffraff in the pit once flung vegetables at him when he ventured out to take a bow. Ask him to tell you the story. I believe he intends to make a play out of his humiliation and call it *Trial by Turnip* or some such nonsense."

"Oh, dear," Jo sighed, "why did you hire him?"

"He was the best we could get on short notice. That is why we are depending on Lizzie to pack the house."

"She will, Terence," Jo assured him. "I know she will. Her voice is magnificent and she works hard. I listen to her sing nearly every day, you know. She never misses a note, let alone a rehearsal."

"If only we could feature her as a solo performer and dispense with everyone else! She would not mind having the stage to herself for five hours, I assure you."

"Perhaps you are right," Josephine said with a smile, "but we must stick to our plan nonetheless. I will do everything I can to make sure that everything is in perfect order."

"There is no such thing as perfection in the theater, Jo. One does one's best, of course, but there is no telling if the audience will like the show. They might walk out. They might throw things. They might demand their money back. Or they might not come at all."

"You are a dreadful pessimist, Terence."

"I have somewhat more experience in these matters than you, my dear sister," he said wearily.

"Well, I cannot wait for the moment when the

great curtain rises!" she exclaimed. "Just think, opening night is only a few weeks away."

"I know," Terence said gloomily.

Upstairs in her own room, Josephine looked through her dresses to find one that would not require her maid's assistance to don.

Her new muslin would do. She pulled it from the clothespress and held it up against herself. The day promised to be warm and the lightness of the dress was entirely suitable.

Airy as it was, it was armor of a sort. Jo was sallying forth to do battle with their various creditors. Of course she would not raise her voice and certainly would not argue. But a pleading look from a young gentlewoman, soft-spoken and well groomed, ought to be enough to melt the heart of the sternest shopkeeper—or so she hoped.

She took a clean chemise and a pair of drawers from a compartment in the clothespress and slipped into both, grateful that she had no need of stays.

The muslin dress, which was decorated with exquisite white embroidery, had been made with an underdress of plainer stuff, in the interest of modesty. She donned both and looked at herself in the cheval glass, pleased with the effect.

Her hair tumbled over her shoulders, uncombed but lustrous in the morning sun. Of course she would not wear it down, but for the moment Josephine let it be.

She wanted to post a letter to her mama when she went out, and she had started it but not finished it last night.

Her brother had seen to it that her room was furnished with everything a young lady might need, including a pretty little desk, painted and carved to look like bamboo. She crossed the room and sat down in its matching chair, taking the precaution of putting on her *robe de chambre* over the clothes she had on. Spots of black ink on a white dress would never do and would never come out in the wash.

She found the half-finished letter in a drawer of the desk and reread what she had written.

My dearest Mama,

I do hope this letter finds you and Papa quite well and happy. I think of you every day and wish you could see how pretty our little house in Guilford Street is. But there is no garden, alas, only a railing about the front. I bought three pots of pansies from the flower seller just to brighten things up and to remind me that spring is on the way, if the rain will ever let up. I am glad that I did, for they remind me of your garden at home. The pansies are being very brave about living in London but I think they would like Richmond far better.

She uncapped the ink bottle and picked up her pen to continue.

I was delighted to have your last letter and to learn that my cousin Penelope will be coming to stay with you and Papa at The Elms. Of course, you have the servants, but that is not the same as the care and attention of a devoted female relation—and I, your only daughter, am far away in London!

It is extraordinarily kind of her, considering that her family is so rich—but then Penelope never seemed to care much for wealth or privilege and she was always very fond of you, Mama. If you wish to visit Bath in her company and take the waters for your health, I know that she will see to your every need.

You mentioned that she is interested in studying the Roman ruins there more than anything else—she was always a scholarly sort of girl. So perhaps she will not be led astray by a handsome young lieutenant on the lookout for an heiress.

Mrs. Shy, who was very kind herself but a stickler for propriety, would be likely to worry about that, Josephine knew. From another drawer, she took out a miniature of her dear mama, painted with exquisite skill upon porcelain. The likeness was very good. It seemed almost as if Mama was about to smile and perhaps chide Jo in her gentle way for looking so disheveled.

Jo mused for a moment upon the very great powers of mothers. Even from a distance, they exerted mysterious influence upon their offspring and could seemingly cast their voices for miles. *Brush your hair. Clean your teeth. Count your blessings. Remember that I love you, dearest child.*

"Yes, Mama," she said aloud. Her mother's favorite saying suddenly came to mind. *And always do the right thing, Jo. Your heart will tell you what that is.*

Josephine sighed. She was not at all sure that she should be doing what she was about to do, but she knew it would help Terence. That alone would please her mother, who could not be in London to look after her son.

She penned a few more lines and blotted the letter, fashioning an envelope for it from a larger piece of paper, which she folded with care. Jo tucked the letter inside but did not seal the envelope.

Perhaps Terence would wish to add a brief note. She did not know whether he had written to their parents recently, but he ought to if he had not. She knew how much her mother enjoyed hearing

from them and suddenly felt a flash of homesick-
ness. She brushed a kiss upon the envelope.

By eleven she had walked all the way to James
Street, just north of Covent Garden. Raised in the
country as she had been, she enjoyed walking, but
the cobblestones made her feet hurt by the time
she reached her destination.

She glanced into the shop windows, noting the
amazing variety of goods for sale in London. One
might find a silversmith next door to a tobacco-
nist's and a haberdasher in the same building as a
purveyor of gingerbread.

Several gentlemen smiled at her, though not in
an unpleasantly forward way, for which she was
grateful. Jo gave in to vanity and assessed her reflection. She had dressed with great care for this
all-important errand and she did look pretty. Her
bonnet was white, like her gown, with pink rib-
bons. A shell-pink shawl was draped over her shoulders. Most becoming of all, a triumphant sparkle
flashed in her eyes.

She had already persuaded the engraver to design and print several thousand tickets without the
expenditure of a single cent. It was fortunate that
the man was a devotee of the divine Miss Loudermilk. Jo had whispered a promise of an introduc-
tion backstage—but after opening night, of course.
She was sure that Lizzie would not mind. After all,
if there were no tickets, there would be no performance.

She continued on, looking for a certain shop
that sold paint, pigments, canvas, varnishes, battens,
light lumber, and everything else that McNeel
needed. He had written down the name of the

shop and its proprietor, Mr. Samuel Picard. She recognized both. She had written to him twice.

Ah, here it was. Jo opened the door and breathed in the now-familiar smell of turpentine as the shop bell jingled above.

The shop was crowded but the other customers were all men. Simply judging by their clothes, she pegged some as artists and others as craftsmen in the building trades. They were preoccupied with the jumble of goods for sale and, for the most part, did not notice her.

Several fellows rummaged through the lumber, looking for straight pieces and rejecting any that looked in the least warped. This seemed to be a matter of sighting down the piece in question to ensure that it was quite straight. She was not sure, dressed as she was, that she could handle such a task on her own and decided to leave it 'til later.

The broad-shouldered shop assistant was busy with a line of customers. Jo was happy enough to stroll through the narrow aisles and investigate the cluttered shelves to her heart's content.

She took McNeel's long list from her reticule and checked off various items with a small pencil, totting up the cost as she moved along. The growing total was alarming. She came to shelves that held long, very heavy rolls of canvas. Frowning, she fingered a scrap hanging from one. Was it sturdy enough? McNeel had not said precisely which sort of canvas was needed.

The shop assistant appeared at the end of the aisle, startling her. "May I help ye find something, miss? That canvas there is our best quality, but not suitable for ladies' dresses. If ye're looking for fine fabrics, there is a mercer three doors down."

"Thank you," Jo said, "but no. The canvas will be

used for stage scenery, and I hoped to find something not too expensive."

He pulled out a different roll from underneath, sending the others rolling about on the shelves.

"This is what ye want, then. And if ye give me the list, I can find the other things right quick. Is this for an amateur theatrical, miss?"

Jo shook her head but said nothing. The man must think that she was putting on a drawing room show for friends and family, and she was not quite prepared to explain the situation.

Of course when she got to the counter, Jo would have to say that she was from the Covent Garden Theater and explain that she was Terence Shy's sister. She planned to arrange for delivery today, and payment upon an unspecified tomorrow, if Samuel Picard was agreeable to that. McNeel had said that Picard was a friendly old fellow and likely to oblige.

She sauntered about the shop, letting the assistant see to gathering up the necessary items and looking out the window to where a lacquered black carriage stood at the curb. She could not see its occupant—not that she cared—but she paused to admire the dappled grays harnessed to it, wondering who owned such a handsome equipage and what he was doing in the not exactly respectable streets near Covent Garden. The owner had to be a man—the sober color of the carriage and its polished brass trim seemed altogether masculine.

A barrow trundled by, pushed by a farm lad who cried his wares, followed by an old woman selling violets from a basket.

Violets. So spring was truly here. Somehow Jo had missed its arrival. Had she been home in the country, she would have been out gathering violets under the trees and making posies for her mother and herself. She felt a pang and turned away from the window just before the man inside the carriage got out.

The assistant waved her over to the counter where Samuel Picard stood, looking over the huge pile of goods. Like his assistant, he was a big man but much older, with bushy white eyebrows and a shrewd expression.

He studied Jo for a few seconds until the shop bell jingled and someone came in. Samuel Picard's rheumy gaze turned in the direction of the new customer and then fixed on Jo again.

"Ye cannot carry all this, my girl. Where is it going to?"

"No," she said, "quite right, I cannot." She bestowed her most gracious smile upon the shopkeeper and hesitated just a moment before adding, "Please deliver it all to Covent Garden. Specifically, to Mr. McNeel, at the stage properties workshop just behind the theater. The door is clearly marked—"

"Aye, miss, that it is. I have been there meself, demandin' payment. So McNeel sent ye, did he? Tell him that he owes me and must give me the money before the end of the week. And what did ye say yer name was? I've not seen ye before."

Josephine scarcely knew how to reply. She could not very well pretend to be someone else, although at the moment she wanted to, desperately. It was one thing to write letters to creditors she had never met and quite another to face them in person. Still, she had not signed them and it was not as if she had incurred the debts. She drew in a deep breath and replied, "Miss Shy. Josephine Shy."

Samuel Picard raised his bushy eyebrows and deep lines appeared on his forehead. He scowled. "Any relation to Mr. Terence Shy?"

"He is my brother."

"Ah, lovely letters he has been sending. But no money."

He crossed his arms over his aproned chest and glared at her sternly. Jo blushed with shame. Nothing in her sheltered life had prepared her for a situation like this. The shop assistant gave her a sympathetic look and turned to his employer.

"Mr. Picard, if I might make a suggestion—"

"Beguiled by those big eyes and soft words, Mick? I am not."

"But sir—" The assistant tried again to placate him, but Picard shut him up with a wave of his meaty hand.

"We will keep the stuff for ye, Miss Shy. But if yer brother orders goods he can't pay for, then he is no better than a common thief. D'ye understand?"

Chapter Seven

Jo stiffened her spine and looked Picard right in the eye. Being made to feel poor and, worse, being treated shabbily for it, was not a pleasant experience. But she did not have to let the shopkeeper or anyone else see how she felt. "Yes, Mr. Picard," she said in a businesslike way. "I will see that payment is made. After all, the show must go on."

"Indeed it must," said a familiar—and very male—voice behind her. "Here is your money, Picard. That ought to cover today's charges and whatever was owing."

The shopkeeper put his big hand over the money Lord Daniel York had placed upon the counter and drew it toward himself. He added it up quickly and nodded.

"Ye're now several shillings ahead. Will there be anything else, miss?"

"You have changed your tune," Lord York said to Picard. There was a slight edge in his voice and an unmistakable steeliness in his gaze as he looked with contempt at the man.

Josephine did not answer the shopkeeper, having turned to face Lord York, unable to do anything save gape at him.

"I saw you enter, Miss Shy. And I overheard this discussion. As I am now a partner in the theater, I consider myself responsible for these expenses."

"But you are not—and you cannot—"

"I can." He smiled down at her. "And I have. Picard, deliver the goods as she asked and be quick about it."

"Yes, sir," the shopkeeper said.

His assistant grinned with relief and winked at Lord York.

Josephine looked down at the counter, not even wanting to wonder what the assistant thought about her relationship to Lord York. So the black carriage was his. She berated herself silently for not recognizing his family crest upon the door.

She understood, of course, that he must have some reason to drive on James Street, as it was so close to the theater, but it seemed an odd coincidence that they had both come to Picard's shop at almost the same time.

As if he could read her mind, he said, speaking quietly, "I shall explain once we are outside." He nodded to Picard and Mick, then guided Jo to the shop door, opening it for her. "Will you walk with me? The theater is not far away and the day is fine."

"Yes," she said, curious to find out why he was here, and grateful that he had saved her from further embarrassment.

He instructed his coachman to take the carriage to an inn and see to the horses. They clip-clopped away, looking very smart, as Jo and Daniel continued on. She looked up at him expectantly and he realized she was waiting for his promised explanation.

"I called at Guilford Street, hoping to see your

brother," he began. *Of course, I hoped to see you as well, Miss Shy.*

Josephine nodded politely.

"But your manservant—do you know, he remembered me from Richmond—told me that Terence had left, and that you were on your way to the theater." *I gave him a guinea for providing that information and he seemed well pleased to have it.* It occurred to Daniel that perhaps Terence had not paid his servants, either.

"And then?" she asked.

"I drove here at once and happened to see you in Picard's window when the coachman stopped at the curb." *And my heart skipped a beat, several beats.* He smiled at her.

Jo smiled back as demurely as she could, feeling altogether unsettled.

He had had just such a smile as a boy . . . open and warm. She remembered it well. It might prove her undoing. If anything, Lord York was even more handsome in the daylight. She had seen him only from a distance on the day when she had followed him about the theater.

His dark good looks were most appealing, and his smile was enhanced by deep dimples. Despite his affable countenance, she felt suddenly safe—there was no other word for it—with him by her side. Lord York was tall and strongly built. A few of the doxies who prowled the streets they were crossing cast longing looks at him and jealous glares at Jo. She ignored them.

"Ye-es," she said nervously, "I visit him there now and then."

"Really, Miss Shy? It seems that you are taking care of business for him as well. Terence gave me the idea that you liked to stay home."

"Oh, I do," she said, "but not always. As you said, the day is very fine."

"But that is not the reason you were in Picard's shop."

"Ah, no," she replied. "Mr. McNeel needed a few small items."

He shook his head. "Hardly a few. The pile on the counter was higher than your shoulders. And very pretty shoulders they are, if you do not mind my saying so."

Lord York looked down, and Jo realized that her shawl was slipping down. She adjusted it at once and drew it tightly around her, hurrying her steps.

"I added things to the list he gave me."

"A brave lie." He shook his head. "Clearly, the plan was to coax what you could from the shopkeeper because the bills were not paid. Most unseemly. Terence should not have sent you to do that."

"But he did not. It was my decision. He has no idea that I am here."

Lord York sighed. "Somehow that is even worse. He ought to look after you with more care. And you ought not to take on such disagreeable tasks, Miss Shy. Surely the younger members of the family should not be more responsible than the older." As the words left his mouth, Daniel realized that he had described his own relationship with his wastrel brother.

Though he would not use the word *wastrel* to describe Terence. No, his dear friend was simply imprudent. Daniel decided not to scold him later, keeping in mind that Terence had cared enough about preserving his sister's reputation to conceal her involvement with the business of running the

Covent Garden Theater. In fact, he had gone out of his way to paint a pretty little picture of a busy bee, happy at home.

"I suppose you think it improper that I spend my days at the theater."

He looked with astonishment at Miss Shy, who was walking so briskly that he had to stride to keep up with her.

"Do you? It is . . . not necessarily improper. Not at all. Although there are many who would think it so, because you are young and a gentlewoman," he answered. "Yet I suppose you have learned much that is, ah, worth learning," he finished up somewhat lamely.

But what had she learned?

The theater was not exactly a finishing academy for genteel young ladies . . . nor was London. Yet, as out of place as she might seem upon its streets, he could not deny that Jo positively glowed, obviously enjoying the hubbub and crowds of the great city. It might not be possible to keep someone so lively at home.

"I am no longer a child, my lord."

I can see that, he thought, thanking the gods of fashion for the popularity of clinging muslin. If anything, the dress she was wearing today did more for her charms than the one he had seen her in while shopping in Richmond with her mother.

"But your brother must still look out for your best interests. It is he who must watch over you, escort you, protect you—"

"Terence does his best," she said.

"Even so." He wondered if he sounded too stern and decided that if he did, it was an excellent way to cover up the emotions that she had stirred in him. Seeing her again so unexpectedly, out and about upon her humble errands, was oddly thrilling. Simply walking with her in this free and easy way made him feel extraordinarily happy. Almost giddy.

He had gone to Guilford Street, if truth be known, hoping to venture onto the unfamiliar terrain of formal courtship, without being exactly sure of how to go about it. It was a very serious business, of course.

That was the plan he had hatched the night he sat staring into the fire, brooding over his loneliness, ensnared by sweet memories and troubled by his amorous thoughts of Miss Shy. He had decided then and there to take the initiative. Be bold and daring. Even go so far as to wangle an invitation to tea with her and her brother.

But chance had intervened. He had been able to come to her rescue in a difficult situation and counted himself lucky for it. He had avoided the deadly dullness of afternoon calls and polite small talk in one swift move and become her hero, if only for five minutes.

Miss Shy turned her face up to his and said something that he didn't hear. Her lips were rosy. Her lips were parted.

How wonderful it would be to kiss her. Right now.

He wondered if he was losing his mind. He ought not to even think about such things. A rational man would not. Josephine did not even know that he remembered her with tenderness. He had mentioned it to her brother, of course, in Miss Loudermilk's dressing room, but only in passing.

Daniel had not told Terence that he intended to court his sister, having not had time to consider every detail as he liked to do. And Lord York prided himself on being a deliberate sort of man.

A proper courtship took time and her father would have to be asked and her mother provided with handkerchiefs of fine linen into which she might cry tears of happiness—Daniel hoped that the news would make Mrs. Shy happy—and then there was the paperwork and all that.

His mind was full of wayward thoughts and wild fancies, shooting up like weeds. Of course it was spring, he told himself . . . and things were thrusting up all over, tulips and the like.

He blamed the incessant rain and the sun that had burst out today for all of it.

Expect the unexpected. Terence had said as much when Lord York first contemplated investing in the theater. A worthy motto and it certainly applied at the moment. He realized that Josephine had paused, no doubt expecting some reply, and he turned his attention to her, hoping that she would continue and he might pick up the thread of what she had been saying.

"It is not Terence's fault that I . . . well, perhaps I am too independent for my own good. I cannot sit still in a drawing room and occupy myself with an embroidery hoop and colored silks for very long."

"No, I did not think so. I remember you loved to be out of doors, rambling in the lanes."

"We all did, back in Richmond," Jo said, a little wistfully.

"Those were happy days, Miss Shy."

They had come to the crooked alley that led to the back door of McNeel's workshop.

"If we go in together, people will talk," she said, looking this way and that.

Daniel saw Molly before Jo did. Slipshod, ill-dressed, her hair uncombed, the dancer stumbled once as she came down the lane, looking as if she'd had a rough night.

A stray cat ran across her path, meowed at her, and disappeared when she cursed at it.

"Too late." He sighed. "There is Molly. Nothing would please her more than spreading gossip about me. No, we must tell your brother that I know you spend your days at the theater and not at home. Yet you have done nothing wrong, of course."

"I should say not," Jo said with indignation.

Molly overheard only the last of their exchange. "Has she done nothing wrong? Ow, our Miss Shy is pure as the driven snow. But p'raps not anymore. Oh, ye're a wicked one, sir!" Molly laughed uproariously and jostled Lord York as she passed. "Excuse me. I am on me way to be fitted for me flyin' harness." She proceeded to the workshop's back door, slamming it shut behind her.

Lord York and Josephine exchanged a look and he shrugged.

"It cannot be helped. Molly will invent a wicked tale about us, circulate it with glee, and then forget all about it. Keep your chin up."

"Very well. No one will believe her anyway. She is a great one for spiteful rumors and petty unkindness." Jo gave him a worried, wondering look. Her eyes were soft with emotion, no doubt the result of two mortifying encounters in a morning, one with that damned shopkeeper and one with Molly.

Ought he to offer manly comfort? And how far should manly comfort go? He put his hands on her shoulders, as if to draw her into his embrace, and then . . . Daniel gave in to a mad impulse, leaned down, and kissed her full on the lips.

He straightened up, looking just as surprised as Jo, and she gasped. "Why did you—oh, my—that was most improper, Lord York!"

"If people are going to talk, we might as well give them something to talk about." He had no idea why he had kissed her, but felt not a particle of regret. He was, of course, ready to marry her in a minute. Not that he would breathe a word of that just yet. She would take him for a madman if he did.

She looked about wildly. The alley was empty. However, someone might have spied them. She had not been paying attention to anything but the delightful sensation of her very first kiss. "Did anyone see us?"

"No."

"Would you mind very much . . . doing it again?"

"Not at all."

Too agitated to think straight, and truly not wanting to give anyone anything to talk about, Jo sent Lord York round to the front of the theater and let herself in the back of McNeel's workshop.

She would have to occupy herself with work immediately, and not think of that extraordinary kiss, or rather, kisses. What had possessed him? Why had she allowed it? What would Molly say?

Do shut up, she told herself. *You enjoyed it.* She could think about it later, when she was not at the theater.

"Mr. McNeel!" she called. "Where are you? Oh, dear, you have gone green all over. I did not see you against the backdrop."

"I am paintin' over Arlecchino's jungle."

"But there is no need. I have persuaded—that is to say, Lord York persuaded—I mean that he paid the bill—at Samuel Picard's shop. We have acres of canvas to work with."

McNeel broke into a greenish grin. "Very good, Miss Shy!"

"It will be delivered today."

He picked up a rag from a basket that overflowed with them and wiped his face. "Then I will leave the tiger where it is. Ye never know what Hugh Newsome will come up with next, and it is not such a bad tiger as all that. I do like the way the eyes glow."

"What about the bears? Or were they dogs? Did we decide?"

McNeel shrugged. "It don't matter. They are already painted out, as ye can see."

He waved a hand at the backdrop she had been looking at all along, and Jo felt like a fool.

"So they are."

"Yer brother wants to see ye, by the way. He is in the theater with Hugh. The auditions for the blacksmiths have begun."

"Thank you, Mr. McNeel, I suppose I must go then. But I did want to let you know that you have what you need."

"Bless your heart." He waved good-bye with the paint-smeared rag and watched her depart.

She entered the theater and saw her brother sitting in a comfortable armchair in one of the boxes nearest the stage. Hugh Newsome sat next to him, whispering into the ear of her . . . her kisser. Lord York was frowning but his face lit up with a tender smile when he saw Jo.

She pressed her lips firmly together.

Surely he had said nothing of the kissing episode to her brother. Would Terence be bound by honor to call him out? She could not imagine her brother fighting a duel. He would probably insist in his whimsical way on feather dusters at thirty paces, and leave it that.

"Jo!" her brother called. "Do come and sit with us. I should like to have your opinion. There are many blacksmiths in the world and many singers, but we cannot seem to find a man who is both."

"Coming," Jo called back. She made her way across the pit to the staircase that led to the boxes.

Terence spotted Tom Higgins in the wings. "Tom! How many more are waiting?"

The stage manager looked behind him and counted on his fingers. "There are three, sir. And the last of them towers over all the others. If the brute can sing, I think ye have yer man."

"I'll be the judge of that," Lizzie Loudermilk said, walking out upon the stage. "I have to sing with him and I will decide."

Terence rolled his eyes heavenward. "Of course, Miss Loudermilk, whatever you say."

Lizzie sniffed. "I am glad that we agree."

Jo entered the box and stood in back just as Terence leaned over to whisper to Lord York. "Daniel, we might as well let her choose."

"Next!" Tom called into the wings.

A very short blacksmith with enormous arms walked onstage. He studied his music, opened his mouth, and sang a particularly sonorous bit, good and loud.

"My, my," Hugh said, "he has a fine voice. And he is able to convey the poignant feeling and the emotional power of my work. This song positively drips with longing."

Terence laughed. "How revolting. No dripping, Hughie, please. Now that the damned rain has stopped and the leaks with it, I don't want to hear that word again."

"Did you ever fix the roof, Terence?" Lord York asked.

Josephine's eyes widened but she said nothing. Surely he would not offer to pay for that. Tom and McNeel had climbed out upon the roof and determined that the whole thing was in need of replacing, not just repair, at horrendous expense.

"No," Terence said. "If we are lucky, it will not rain again until after opening night. Then we can fix it, if we have the money."

"You cannot run a theater on luck," Lord York began, "and as far as the money, I really ought to examine the books—" He was interrupted by a halloo from the stage.

"Mr. Shy!" boomed Lizzie in the direction of their box. "This blacksmith will not do!"

"Excuse me, Daniel. Why not, Lizzie?" Terence called back.

"Open your eyes. The man is a head shorter than I am."

"But he can sing!" Hugh cried.

"He can't play the part on stilts, Hughie dear. Not when he has to pick me up."

Miffed, the dramatist said nothing more and slumped in his armchair.

"Jo, do you not agree?" Lizzie called. "Mr. Shy, is your sister with you? Jo! Jo! Come out, come out, wherever you are."

Terence turned to look toward the back of the box. "Oh—hello. Do sit with us. Take the chair on the other side of Daniel, that's a good girl."

Good girl? If only her brother knew what had happened in the alley. But he didn't. Molly must not have had a chance to tittle-tattle.

As she walked to the chair by Lord York, Jo reflected on the odd fact that being a little bad could feel deliciously good. She sat down, folding her hands primly in her lap and refusing to look at him. Considering what had happened only moments ago, she thought it best to concentrate all her attention on the stage.

Lizzie awaited another singing swain, with her hands on her hips and a scowl on her face. "Next victim," she called to the stage manager. "Keep them coming, Tommy."

Another fellow edged out from the wings. He was tall, thin, and stooped. He took one look at Lizzie and dropped his music, then tripped over his feet as he tried to retrieve the pages.

"Oh, no," growled Lizzie. "Next!"

"You haven't even heard him," Hugh said rather peevishly. "Give the poor man a chance."

Lizzie shrugged. "He can barely pick up pieces of paper. How is he going to carry me over the threshold of the cottage when we sing our duet? The fellow is spindly, not like a blacksmith at all. He won't do either."

The thin man gave her a reproachful look, and slunk away.

"There is one more. Says he is a real blacksmith, too. Harry Longwood, step forth," Tom said, looking into the wings.

A gigantic man answered his summons and strode onto the stage. The theater reverberated with each of his steps, and the group in the box sat up straight. Hugh leaned forward on the balcony rail, resting his head on his folded arms.

"Oo!" said Lizzie with evident satisfaction. "Now we're getting somewhere." She came forward to look him over.

Harry Longwood stood as staunchly as if he had been carved from English oak, his massive arms folded over a very broad chest.

It was easy to imagine him in a leather apron, wielding a huge hammer with all his might, forging red-hot iron in a shower of brilliant sparks. His thighs seemed ready to burst from his tight breeches, and his neck was a thick column of muscle, springing from shoulders that were impossibly wide.

He looked Lizzie right in the eye, unmoving, even when she boldly put a hand on his chest.

"Oo! Like a brick wall!"

He made no reply.

She moved her hand to the thick, curly hair on his head, stretching up to run her fingers through it. "Oo! Taller than I am, too. Why, he makes me feel like a kitten." She caressed his rugged jaw and moved closer.

She seemed to be—Jo strained to hear—yes, Lizzie was purring in his ear.

The man grinned as if it tickled but still made no reply.

"He'll do, Mr. Shy," she said, stepping back with a huge smile on her face.

"You haven't heard him sing!"

"Oh, right. Go ahead, tra-la-la to your heart's content, Mr. Longwood." She picked up a few sheets of music from the floor and thrust them into his hands. "But my mind is made up, Terence. He is a real man and no mistake."

The man nodded, cleared his throat, and rattled the sheets of music.

"Need a note?" Lizzie asked. She sang out high and clear and strong. *Laaaaaaaa.*

The man cleared his throat again and let out a note that matched hers perfectly. *Laaaaaaa.*

Lizzie cast a worried look at him. "What was that squeak?" she asked. "Is there a mouse in the house? That can't be your voice."

"It is, madam," the blacksmith replied in a dignified, high-pitched voice. "I am a counter-tenor."

Her face fell. "And I was expecting a bass."

"We all were," Terence whispered after a minute.

The group in the box was convulsed with silent laughter. "I fear that this brawny blacksmith has suffered a dreadful injury. It is a dangerous trade. Poor fellow."

Hugh shook his head. "I don't think so. I happened to glimpse Longwood at the piss-pots backstage—I beg your pardon, Miss Shy, but I must speak frankly. He is, uh, entire. As much of a man as a man can be."

Lizzie was walking about the stage looking rather agitated. "May I speak to you privately, Mr. Shy?"

"Of course, Miss Loudermilk." He turned to the dramatist. "Hugh, come with me and chat with Longwood while Lizzie and I have it out. I have an idea but she might not like it."

Their departure left Jo and Lord York alone. True, they were in full view of the people on the stage and anyone who might wander into the box. But they were out of earshot and could talk with perfect freedom—if she seemed inclined to talk, which she was not. They sat some minutes in uneasy silence.

He glanced her now and then, thinking about what he might say. At last he spoke, in a calm, measured tone that gave no hint of his inner agitation. "Forgive me, Miss Shy. I should not have kissed you."

"A kiss is just a kiss."

That was not the response he had expected. She sounded . . . positively blasé. He wondered again, feeling annoyed, just what she had learned in this damned theater.

"Did you, um, enjoy the experience?" he asked.

"I did," Jo said, still refusing to look at him.

Lord York was immediately heartened. So she

was not blasé about *his* kisses, just kisses in general. Still, he thought it best to stick to apologizing.

"Then I should not have kissed you more than once."

"Pshaw. I asked you to," she said lightly.

"So you did, Miss Shy."

"And did *you* enjoy the experience, Lord York?"

He had certainly not expected a question like that. Yet he was not fooled by her worldly air, which seemed put on somehow, as if she had learned lines and was merely playing a part. Was she doing it to attract him or to keep him at a distance? Lord York could not, at the moment, decide upon an answer to that subtle question. "Yes, very much," he said hastily, "but decency requires that I—"

"Decency be damned," she said with the faintest trace of a smile upon her pretty lips.

"Miss Shy! Wherever did you pick up that expression?"

"Lizzie—I mean Miss Loudermilk."

Lord York raised one eyebrow. "I see. And do you assist Miss Loudermilk as well as your brother? Terence did not tell me that, either."

"I do."

She *still* would not look at him. Lord York saw the color rise in her cheeks. He understood the cause of her blushing embarrassment. "Ah, that explains much. Miss Loudermilk is hardly a proper friend for a modest young gentlewoman."

She turned at last and glared at him. "Whatever do you mean? I suppose a prig might consider Miss Loudermilk disreputable, but she is a good soul with a warm heart."

"Of course," he said hastily, wondering whether Jo thought of him as priggish. "Yes, she is, in her way. But your reputation . . . Oh, Miss Shy, what I did was enough to compromise you."

She only shrugged. "If you are worried about that, I do not consider myself compromised and no one was looking." She hoped she sounded sophisticated. "It was an amusing interlude but it meant nothing to me."

He sighed in a deeply unhappy way. Another minute passed in which neither of them spoke.

Perhaps, Josephine thought, she had sounded merely heartless. She remembered how gallant he had been when coming to her rescue in Picard's shop and began to feel ashamed of her flippant reply.

"Is that true, Jo? I had hoped otherwise," he said at last.

"Hoped for what? Please explain. I find that I am thoroughly confused." *And that I am wildly attracted to you as well.* Jo wondered what explanation he would offer. But she could not imagine having to explain her own actions—most of all, why she had kissed him back and asked for another. It had seemed like the thing to do at the time, of course.

"Ah . . . where to begin?" he said slowly.

"Just begin. Perhaps it will make sense when and where we least expect it."

He cleared his throat. "I, uh, was most happy to hear from Terence that you were living with him in London. I knew that—I hoped that—I would see you again. I was not expecting that to happen at a shopkeeper's counter, of course."

"Yet it did."

"It is a good thing that you like to shop. It was not long ago that I drove through the village and saw you doing just that with your mother, Jo. You had a basket over your arm and wore a bonnet that was very pretty and at that moment I knew—I mean to say that I felt—oh, never mind. I was about to say something nonsensical and romantic."

"I see." She could have accused him of following her, then and now, but since she had followed him on his first day in the theater, decided against it. "Well, perhaps you shouldn't."

He gave her a yearning look but she turned her head away, seizing upon the silence that fell between them to think about things.

After Terence's departure for London, Lord York had not once visited The Elms. But he had remembered her. She knew that much from hearing him say so while she was hiding in Lizzie's closet.

His mother had talked to Jo about him now and again, and of his father's death after a long illness, his brother coming into the title. Her own dear mama had called Gerald a worthless blackguard—strong language indeed for the old lady. Mrs. Shy thought it most unfair that Daniel, the dutiful son, had to struggle so to make his mark in the world.

Terence had not offered much information on the reasons for their unlikely partnership, but it occurred to her suddenly that Lord York was no longer as grand nor as rich as she had naively assumed.

And it was clear, despite his awkward apology for kissing her, that he was not always as proper as he thought he ought to be. Huzzah for that, she thought. Considering that the cat was now out of the bag and he knew that she assisted her brother and Miss Loudermilk . . . Oh, dear, it was a bottomless bag, filled with cats, and she would not be able to keep them inside if he was to spend as much time as Jo did at the theater.

Had her brother not said that Lord York might be *too* good? Certainly he did not seem the sort of man who went about kissing women willy-nilly. Or was he?

Jo cast a sideways look at Daniel, and was surprised to see an expression of schoolboy melancholy upon his handsome face. He was eight years older, well born and well bred, and had lived in London for years. Though she had no one to compare him to, it seemed to her that he kissed with sensual skill. He probably had more experience with the physical side of things but perhaps had yet to fall in love.

She, of course, had no experience whatsoever with *les affaires de coeur*. Love and its many splendors were mostly a mystery to her as yet. But Jo could claim that she had researched the subject in depth, thanks to romance novels, which she bought on the sly, read by the dozen, and gave away to her younger female relations.

She had even bequeathed a few of the racier titles to her cousin Penelope, the family scholar of antiquities. Penelope had read them with an air of puzzlement, saying that she did not see what was particularly thrilling about things like kisses and fond embraces. Jo had felt that it would be a waste of time to explain just why she thought such things were probably wonderful.

And now Jo knew exactly why. Lord York's masterful kisses were the very stuff of which romance novels were made. That they had been bestowed in a cobblestone alley in back of a theater was, however, not quite right. Romance heroines were usually kissed upon moonlit balconies or in gilt carriages or the like, as far as she knew.

If she had to guess, she would say that Lord York had fallen in love, for no very good reason. And if she had to confess, she knew that she might be in love with him, also for no very good reason. Thus far, their story was very like a romance novel. But exactly how it would end up remained to be seen.

At the moment, Lizzie was screaming her head off onstage.

Chapter Eight

"Lizzie, no!" Jo cried. She had run down the stairs in back of the boxes and onto the stage, leaving Lord York behind. "You will look a fright if you don't stop!"

Frustrated and utterly furious, the singer was nervously pulling at her red mane, tangling it in a way that would defy a comb and Dora's best efforts, Jo knew.

"Fetch Ginny!"

"I am right here," the wardrobe mistress said quietly, walking out from the wings. "What are ye howling about?"

Lizzie flung herself down upon a green-carpeted hill done up with fake flowers. "They won't let me have the big blacksmith!"

Ginny sighed. "Ye sound like a child screamin' for a toy."

"And a very nice toy he is, Ginny. I want him."

The wardrobe mistress looked into the wings. "Well, he is still here, talking to Mr. Shy and Hugh. And he certainly seems to be a real man, as ye said, for all that he has such a high voice."

"He is magnificent. We are perfect together. He makes me and my big bum look . . . tiny."

"Now, Lizzie," Ginny chided, "the audience comes to hear ye sing, not to look at yer bum. The men do look at yer bosom, though."

"Not as if anyone could miss either," Lizzie said indignantly.

"P'raps not. But no one will believe that ye've magically grown smaller just because ye're singing with a great strapping man. And they don't care what size ye are, Liz."

Lizzie rolled over on the hill, trying to look at her bum. "I think it is bigger. The script calls for a blacksmith who can lift me and Harry Longwood is the only man who can."

"Still, he does not *sound* manly, Lizzie," Jo said. She joined Lizzie on the carpeted hill and resisted the temptation to tug at the fake grass and pick the paper daisies.

"I don't care."

"The crowds will laugh if it sounds like two women singing."

"I don't care."

Ginny looked into the wings. "Here they come. Hush, you two. Perhaps our Mr. Shy has come up with a solution."

Terence peeked out from behind the curtain. "Has Lizzie stopped that fearful shrieking for good? Or is she just resting between fits?"

"She has stopped," Ginny replied. "Blessed silence prevails."

"Then I will get to the point." He came out into the light. "Lizzie, we have decided to cast Harry Longwood in the part of the blacksmith."

The counter-tenor strode forth and towered over Terence. "I consider myself honored to sing on the same stage with Miss Loudermilk."

Jo ducked her head to hide a smile. It would take her a while to get used to a fluty voice like that coming from such a big man, but she knew she had to. She looked up to see whether Lord York was still in the box and saw that he too was suppressing a smile.

"But you will not actually *be* singing, Harry—may I call you Harry?" Terence asked. "The, ah, discrepancy between your voice and your appearance simply is not right for the role."

"Then what will I be doing?" Longwood asked, looking disappointed.

"I shall think of something," Lizzie said, casting an admiring look at his powerful physique.

"Lizzie, shut up." That was Ginny, who smiled nonetheless.

"You will merely pretend to sing, Mr. Longwood. And Fred, one of our satyrs, a little fellow with a remarkably deep voice, will stand behind a screen and sing your part. Fred will be able to see you, of course, and so you will seem to sing every note. But the audience will not see him. It is a trick that requires a great deal of practice but it has been done—many times."

"Very well," Longwood replied. "When do rehearsals begin?"

"At once." Terence grinned at Lizzie. "No more lolling about, Miss Loudermilk."

She gave him a regal wave of dismissal and went right on lolling.

"Harry, Mr. Newsome is waiting for you backstage," said Terence. "He will find Fred for you, and you can rehearse in the downstairs studio."

"Thank you, Mr. Shy. This will be my stage debut, you know. Mother Longwood will be so proud."

"She will be the only member of the audience who knows that you are mouthing the words of the song. The ushers must not seat her next to the critics. What if she gives the secret away?"

"She would never," Harry said, seemingly shocked at the thought.

"Good, good, glad to hear it." Terence patted the blacksmith on his mighty shoulder, and the big man left.

Tom Higgins came out, dragging a table of light wood, painted to look like wrought iron, and two iron chairs.

"What are you doing, Tom?"

"These is for *The Shepherdess*. The scene at the rustic inn where the lovers sup," he replied. "We must test the lighting. Hugh wants it all soft and pink. Says someone gets seduced."

"Really?" Terence asked, giving Lizzie an arch look. "Who could it be?" He consulted the script and read aloud. " 'Our heroine, the trembling virgin, cuts slices from a succulent ham and feeds them to her muscular lover.' Will we need a real ham, Tom?"

The stage manager nodded. "Don't see how you could use a papier-mâché one, not if she's feeding him bits of it. And it ain't like our Lizzie is a real virgin."

"I should say not. Get a good ham, Tom. It will help Harry keep his strength up," Lizzie said. She rose somewhat awkwardly from the carpeted hill, and Josephine scrambled to her feet as well.

"It seems an unnecessary expense to have a fresh ham each night, but if we must . . ." Terence let his sentence trail off.

"Ye can let the bit players and dancers finish it," Tom said loudly. "They are hungry enough to fight over a bone, since they still have not been paid, Mr. Shy. Nor have I."

Josephine looked up at Lord York again. His expression was quite serious. She supposed that, having heard Tom's complaint, he would now insist on looking at the books, as her brother had surmised. She hoped he would not encounter too many unpleasant surprises.

Yet the Covent Garden Company needed a steady hand at the helm. She had not realized that until the moment of truth in Samuel Picard's shop. Writing letters for Terence to sign and send off to Picard and all the others had been almost a game at first, but not anymore.

The livelihoods of many people depended on the company's ability to pay what they owed to their players and their creditors. As rude as the shopkeeper had been, he was right. True, Terence had been plagued by bad luck, but it was clear enough that he had no head for money. She did not want to see him end up in debtor's prison.

If Daniel could teach her dear brother to be more prudent and preserve Terence from that dreadful indignity, she would be eternally grateful.

They needed him. She *was* glad he was here, looking after things, like a guardian angel . . . and provider of heavenly kisses in unexpected places. She would not mind more of those. And if it happened that he really was in love with her, then it all might work out very well.

Jo caught Lord York's eye and favored him with a dazzling smile. Even from here, she could see him blush.

He was a bit of a prig. But he was very kind all the same, she thought. She turned her attention back to her brother, who was talking to Tom in a low voice, and then looked about for something to do, ignoring Lord York for the moment.

Precisely why Jo had smiled at him like that after their somewhat prickly conversation, Daniel did not know. It made his face grow warm. He reflected again upon the very odd things that seemed to happen to him inside—and just outside—this damned theater. Everything seemed subject to change in an instant, as if a capricious magician bent on mischief were in charge.

Lord York knew that he had behaved in a way utterly out of keeping with his character or good intentions.

Now that he was alone in the box and Jo upon the stage, busily rearranging the table and chairs that Tom had brought out, he reflected again upon what he had done. He had just kissed the sister of his good friend and business partner—in the alley, where anyone might have seen them. Yet he had not been able to resist the impulse to do so.

Certainly Jo had grown into a young woman of compelling charm. He would have to admit that, for whatever reason—the advent of spring, the thrusting of tulips, the spells of unseen magicians, the innocent parting of a rosy mouth—he was smitten with her. Yet he ought to have been able to restrain himself, and stick to his plan of courting her properly. Why had he been so impetuous? He could not answer that question.

Perhaps he should confine himself to the fact that he had enjoyed the kiss—well, kisses. Very much. And so had Jo. She had said so, rather boldly.

There was no doubt in Daniel's mind that Miss Loudermilk was partly to blame for Josephine's forward manner. The singer's bawdy jokes and unladylike behavior were not a good influence, but it was not his place to tell Josephine that. Still, if her brother was too preoccupied to watch over her, he himself would have to. Discreetly, of course.

He looked down at the stage again. Jo seemed to be laughing helplessly at something Lizzie had said, and Ginny was laughing as well. But what harm was there in such fun?

For all her pretense of sophistication and light words, he knew perfectly well that Jo was still innocent. A wanton would not have kissed him back with such quivering eagerness, as if the experience was entirely new to her. She had seemed to melt in his arms.

But he must not give in to mere desire. She deserved to be wooed and won and wed. Properly. Formally. Eternally.

His imagination skipped ahead to the best part: sweeping her off her feet with passionate abandon and carrying her in his loving arms to his bed. His mind began to fill in the delicious details of the—

"Seduction scene!" he heard Terence yell. Lord York sat bolt upright with a gasp.

He leaned forward in the box to listen to the conversation on the stage and sighed with relief. Terence was talking to the stage manager about the play.

He ought to go down and not sit alone in the empty box, indulging in romantic fantasies. He decided to join them.

"Tom, do you need someone onstage while you try out different effects?" Terence asked.

"It would 'elp," Tom said.

Lizzie sauntered off to the wings with one arm slung around Ginny's shoulders. "Don't look at me. I am going to my dressing room for a lie-down.

I shall need to keep my own strength up. Harry Longwood is coming by for tea before the evening rehearsal."

Ginny snorted.

"While I am sleeping, Ginny, it would be very nice if you would go out and fetch some cakes. I am famous for my hospitality, you know."

"Is that what you call it, Lizzie?"

The two friends left through the corridor, and the sound of their banter soon faded.

Terence looked at his sister. "Jo, that leaves you to stand in for Lizzie. Are you ready to ruin your reputation at last?"

"Whatever do you mean?"

"I was only joking. But Tom needs someone to sit at this table while we work on the lighting. No one is watching, and therefore it cannot be said that you have gone on the stage, even if you are on the stage."

"I think I understand."

"Then please sit down." Terence pulled out a chair for his sister. "Ah, hello, Daniel. I was wondering when you would come down from the box and join us. Are you ready to examine the books— it is deadly dull work, I assure you—or would you like to keep Jo company?"

She gave him another damned dazzling smile.

Lord York sat down in the other chair.

"Closer, Daniel."

"What?"

"Move your chair next to hers. You two need to be quite close. This is a—"

"Seduction scene," Lord York said stiffly. He did not meet Josephine's gaze.

"Very good!" Terence exclaimed. "So you were paying attention. And I thought you were just daydreaming."

"I never do, Terence."

"More's the pity. Daydreaming is a blissful occupation and very good for you, you know."

"I beg your pardon?"

"Oh, never mind," Terence said affably. "I suppose I do too much of it, eh?"

"Aye," Tom said.

"What? Where were we, Tom? And what are you doing with that little snipping thing?"

"Trimmin' the lampwicks, sir. There, done. And now for the effects."

Lord York watched as the two of them picked through various screens used to cast a tinted light upon the stage, and leaned a few against the wall. Jo seemed disinclined to talk at the moment. He could not think of a word to say himself and looked out at the vast, empty theater.

He would concentrate upon the business at hand and not think about anything amorous. Perhaps he would count the seats.

There were far too many. Covent Garden Theater held three thousand.

He could not quite imagine what the appreciative applause of six thousand hands sounded like to performers onstage. He supposed it was thrilling.

But if that same three thousand did not like the play, or the pantomime of the nymphs and satyrs, or the singing castaway, the house would erupt with hisses and catcalls and flying vegetables.

The thought was sobering. Everything had to be made ready by opening night, and made to the highest standards of theatrical craft. Lord York was not sorry he had covered the expenditure for McNeel's materials.

Instead of counting the seats, he began to do sums in his head, something he had always found calming. *Approximately three thousand people at such-*

and-such number of shillings per ticket equaled . . . quite a lot. Damnation. His thoughts were more jumbled than before. Having Jo so close—their chairs were almost touching—was much more interesting arithmetic. *One plus one equaled . . . two happy hearts.*

He fought to control his wayward thoughts once more, casting about in his mind for a surefire squasher of moony feelings. He hit upon accounting. There was nothing at all moony about accounting. The numbers added up or they did not.

He suspected that Terence's numbers never did. Perhaps money was being wasted in one area that might be better spent in another. Certainly it was imperative that the players receive their back wages as soon as possible.

If he had to pay them as well from his own pocket, it was worth it. Despite Terence's airy reassurances, a hambone once a week divided among the cast would not suffice.

He saw Jo give her brother an adoring, affectionate look, and frowned slightly. He would have to be careful not to offend Terence or accuse him of mismanagement. His old friend was clearly better suited to the creative side of running a theater.

Daniel looked out again in the cavernous theater, then turned to Jo. She seemed to be studying him. He hoped his profile was sufficiently noble from her point of view, and then realized that he was thinking like an actor, something he would never want to be.

He blamed the silly thought upon the unseen magician he had imagined. *Some* sort of mysterious hocus-pocus was wreaking havoc with Lord York's ability to reason. If only he knew what it was.

"What are you thinking, Lord York?"

"That . . . um . . . I don't know what I was thinking. My brain feels rather foggy."

"Oh, dear. Should I send someone out to the coffeehouse? Or would you prefer tea? There are cups among the props that we could use."

She turned and rose halfway, looking for a stage-hand, he supposed.

"No, Jo, not now," Terence called. "Stay where you are."

"Thank you anyway," Daniel said. "I will be all right. I suppose I think too much."

"Like my brother, perhaps you have too much to think about," Jo said softly, "and too much work to do."

"True enough, Miss Shy. Yet we all must work together to make the show a success." He gestured to the empty boxes and rows of benches. "We have a great many seats to fill."

Terence bustled back onto the stage. "At the moment, all I care about is these two seats. So. Here are our young lovers . . . oh, do not narrow your eyes like that, Daniel, I meant nothing by it. Let us see how they look in a rosy, romantic light."

Jo could just see Tom holding a framed piece of sheer pink material in front of a row of backstage lamps.

"Oh, very nice. Now do you think we could add a breeze? If the flowers on the carpeted hill sway a little, it will add a touch of verisimilitude."

"A touch of what?" Tom called. "Blimey, I don't think we have any. Ask McNeel. He has vermilion, I know, and verdigris, but I don't know about that there verisimilitude."

"It is not paint, Tom. It means a lifelike touch. If those damned daisies stand up too straight, they do not look real."

"Bring on the bellows!" Tom called. "Himself wants a breeze!"

A stagehand appeared, dragging a contraption

that did indeed resemble a very large fireplace bellows, supported by an open frame. The stagehand began to operate it and the thing let out an asthmatic wheeze.

"Dear me, it *is* noisy. We shall have to strike up the violins at that point."

"Lot of work just to make daisies move," Tom grumbled.

Terence gave him a lofty look. "God is in the details, or so they say." He waved to the stagehand. "Try it again, if you please."

The stagehand operated the device with greater vigor than before and it blew much harder, flattening the poor little daisies and causing Jo to clutch her skirt to keep it from flying up. She exchanged a look and an embarrassed laugh with Daniel, who smoothed down his ruffled hair.

"No, no!" Terence said crossly. "I want a gentle zephyr, not a damned gale."

The stagehand nodded. After several more tries, he produced a satisfactory breeze and was permitted to drag the machine away. Terence went back to the problem of the lights, while Daniel twiddled his thumbs.

He could not be expected to sit right next to the object of his affections if her skirt was to fly up. God only knew what he might feel compelled to do next. He might very well kiss her in front of her brother, given sufficient provocation.

"I am not certain this is the best use of my time, Terence. I had planned to look at the books today."

"To hell with the books. Look into her eyes," Terence said. "I am trying to block the scene and set the order of the changes in light for it."

"That is all very well, but I do not see why—"

"Look into her eyes!"

Feeling foolish, Lord York turned to Jo and did as he was bid. Her eyes were a beautiful mixture of blue and green, with a mischievous sparkle.

"Do not be embarrassed," she whispered. "It is only make-believe."

Not at all, he wanted to say.

"Jo, be still. Tom, can we get the light to fall directly on her face?"

"I think so." The stage manager fiddled with other screens and lights for a minute until the desired effect was achieved.

"Lovely. Jo, you look positively radiant."

She propped her pretty chin on one hand and stuck out her tongue at her brother. It glowed pink in the artificial light.

Lord York forced himself to look away.

"Now pretend to feed him bits of ham."

"May I have a pretend ham, brother dear?"

"Just pantomime the action, if you please. Feed him tenderly, as if he were a baby."

Lord York opened his mouth to protest, then shut it again. The books could wait, he supposed.

Jo picked up an imaginary knife and fork, and carved an imaginary ham. Picking up nothing with her fingertips, she brought them to Lord York's lips.

"Open moufy," she whispered, giggling. "Be my baby."

Dear God. The tenderness in her tone sapped his strength. But he parted his lips ever so slightly. She popped in the imaginary tidbit. He pretended to chew, which was not easy, considering that he wanted to laugh at his predicament. Or howl with frustration.

His ludicrous expression made Jo giggle even more.

"Splendid," Terence said. "Well played, you two. Daniel, would you like to understudy the blacksmith?"

Lord York looked at him with horror. "Certainly not. Terence, I really must get some work done. I am happy to help you here, of course, but when will you finish?"

Terence seemed not to hear the question and spoke to his sister. "Jo, feed him again. I would like to add a touch of purple to the light and see how that looks."

"Purple, eh? That's for passion." Molly's braying voice came from the wings. She strolled onstage, still in the disreputable clothes she had worn on the street, with a looking-for-trouble gleam in her eyes. "Are his lordship and our Miss Shy playin' the rustic lovers now?"

"Of course not," Terence said, once again preoccupied with the lights.

The dancer put her hands on her hips. "They have had practice. I saw them in the alleyway right in back of the theater. Alone."

"What of it?" Terence replied.

Jo, who had been expecting this to happen, was quite relieved that her brother did not seem in the least interested in Molly's innuendos.

"Be off, Molly," Tom said contemptuously. "And don't gossip about your betters."

She turned on the cracked heel of her street shoe and gave them all a haughty stare. "But his lordship wanted to give people something to talk about."

Lord York turned scarlet and exchanged a guilty look with Jo but he did not reply. Molly tossed him an arch look and walked out.

"Did you really say that, Daniel?" Terence asked. "What were you doing in the alley?"

"We were, ah, feeding stray cats," Josephine said suddenly. At the moment, she did not want to tell Terence that she had gone to Samuel Picard's shop without his permission or that Lord York had paid for McNeel's supplies. She would, but not now. Certainly she would never tell her brother that his friend had kissed her. More than once.

"Oh, well, I suppose people might talk about that. There are enough rats running around Covent Garden to feed a thousand stray cats. No one but my soft-hearted sister would ever think of giving them more to eat."

Terence said nothing else. Josephine was puzzled by her brother's nonchalance but grateful for it all the same.

Lord York rose from the table. "You must excuse me. I find that playacting makes me hungry. But I will have something sent in and I will eat my lunch in the office. And if you don't mind, Terence, I will begin to examine the books as I had planned."

"Not at all," Terence said, "swot away."

Lord York made a slight bow to Josephine. "Miss Shy, it has been a pleasure. And thank you for the imaginary ham."

"The pleasure was mine," she said, looking as demure as she could. She watched him walk through the door that was set into the proscenium arch and close it behind him.

Her brother sent the stage manager away on some errand and studied her for a moment. "How prim you look. Feeding strays in the alley, eh? You will have a pack of starving tabbies following you about if you keep that up."

"I suppose you don't believe me."

"I have much more important things on my mind. The lights and the blocking are only the beginning. But I appreciate your willingness to play along, Jo. You do seem to like Daniel and I needed to stall him."

She gave her brother a sharp look. "I did not realize you were stalling him."

Terence shrugged. "I am not at all sure that I want him to look at the books. But he is my partner and I cannot say no."

"Let him help you, Terence."

"I suppose I must." He sighed. "Do you know, I never expected that putting on plays would be so exhausting. Or that I would be working almost without stopping, seven days a week."

"I find that I am never bored."

"Indeed, that is scarcely possible in the wonderful world of the theater," her brother replied. There was a sarcastic edge in his voice. "The players are a rowdy lot and cheeky to a fault. Molly is the worst. I am not sure I should have given her a solo."

"No one else would have the nerve to fly about the stage."

"No, I suppose not. Not without a lucky chicken bone or some such charm to protect them, anyway. Superstition seems to be their religion."

Jo, remembering the faded garter that Lizzie still kept from her first perfomance, nodded in agreement.

"They would rather sleep on Sunday than go to church. Oh, the theater is a den of iniquity."

"Don't be silly, Terence."

"But the members of our company delight in behaving badly," he went on. "Do you know, I cannot keep up with who is in or out of love with whom. They are quite free with their affections."

"I could make a list for you and note the changes daily," she said.

"Certainly not. It would only mean more jealous fights."

Josephine nodded. "I hope no one casts a longing glance at Harry Longwood. Lizzie would be quite put out."

"Well, she would win in the end. Lizzie brooks no rivals."

"That's true," Jo said.

"I suppose I would hear at once if anyone attempts to take the blacksmith from her. They are all dreadful gossips. And backstabbers. It is not only a den of iniquity, it is a hotbed of vice. Have I forgotten to mention any?"

"You left out the intrigues," Jo said. "And don't forget the spying."

"Oh, dear, I should not have told you quite so much. You are in danger of losing your innocence."

"Oh, that. Long gone. Haven't missed it. I am enjoying myself immensely."

Terence stretched his legs a bit by walking around the stage. "Do you think that the show will be a hit, Jo? I cannot see the forest for the trees at this point."

"It will all come together by opening night."

"When? How? There seems to be no end to the confusion. Every single performer in today's rehearsals missed a cue or two."

"But Lizzie is in fine fettle and she seems very pleased with Harry Longwood."

"I fear she will wear him out."

Jo gave him a suitably shocked look.

"Forgive me. I meant upon the stage."

"So long as she is happy, she will do justice to Hugh's songs. They are rather better than the play part," she said tactfully.

"I would agree. Our distinguished dramatist is a pompous ass who devotes five hours a day to sharpening pencils and five minutes to writing. But he is not bad at songs."

"Count your other blessings. The crew works hard. McNeel is a treasure."

"That's true, Jo, and so is Ginny Goodchurch. How she puts up with Miss Loudermilk, I do not know."

"They have been friends for a very long time," Jo pointed out.

"Yes, they have gone from show to show together over the years, and Tom Higgins with them."

"His stagehands are like his soldiers," Jo said.

Terence grinned. "I suppose you could say that Signor Arlecchino has become the loose cannon in that army. One never seems to know what he will do next or where he will turn up. And is that not his voice now?"

She turned at the sound of faint shrieks of laughter echoing down a nearby corridor and the clamor of an energetic pursuit. Jo recognized Molly's bray and frowned. An exuberant male voice shouting in Italian mingled with hers.

Within seconds, Molly dashed back onto the stage, with Arlecchino hot on her heels. "Ow, Mr. Shy! He won't leave me alone!"

They were not about to stop. The dancer and Arlecchino kept right on running.

"Oh, dear. Molly is in love again," Terence said, craning his neck to see which way they had gone.

"I am happy for her," Jo said.

"Why? I should think you would dislike her for telling tales about you and Lord York. She has a malicious streak."

"True. But that is neither here nor there, my dear brother. However, if Molly is in love with Signor Arlecchino, that will give people something else to talk about."

He gave her a level look. "Besides you and Lord

We'd Like to Invite You to Subscribe to Zebra's Regency Romance Book Club and Send You 4 Free Books as Your Introduction! (Worth $19.96!)

If you're a Regency lover, imagine the joy of getting 4 FREE Zebra Regency Romances and then the chance to have these lovely stories delivered to your home each month at the lowest price available! Well, that's our offer to you and here's how you benefit by becoming a Regency Romance subscriber:

- *4 FREE Introductory Regency Romances are delivered to your doorstep (you only pay for shipping & handling)*
- *4 BRAND NEW Regencies are then delivered each month (usually before they're available in bookstores)*
- *Subscribers save almost $4.00 off the cover price every month*
- *You also receive a FREE monthly newsletter, which features author profiles, discounts, subscriber benefits, book previews and more*
- *There's no risks or obligations...in other words, you can cancel whenever you wish with no questions asked*

Join the thousands of readers who enjoy the savings and convenience offered to Regency Romance subscribers. After your initial introductory shipment, you'll receive 4 brand-new Zebra Regency Romances each month to examine for 10 days. Then, if you decide to keep the books, you pay the preferred subscriber's price, plus shipping and handling.

It's a no-lose proposition, so return the FREE BOOK CERTIFICATE today!

ll

REGENCY ROMANCE BOOK CLUB

Zebra Home Subscription Service, Inc.

P.O. Box 5214

Clifton NJ 07015-5214

PLACE
STAMP
HERE

York, you mean. *Is* there something to talk about, Jo?"

She turned pinker than she had under the stage light. "No."

Terence sighed. "What a pity."

Chapter Nine

And a few weeks later . . .

Lord York had sent his carriage to fetch Jo and Ginny home. Jo could just see the black gleam of it through the trees and shrubberies. He had thought a visit to the physick garden of Chelsea would do them good, and Ginny had begged to go, as she needed to buy dried lavender from its shop to freshen the costumes.

And Jo, in Lord York's opinion, had needed fresh air. She had not even wanted to argue. He had not accompanied them, being too busy. The ongoing rehearsals were longer and more chaotic than ever, and Terence had turned over most of the theater's business management to his friend in order to concentrate upon the show.

Her brother grumbled that the Almighty had created the entire world with less trouble in a mere seven days, and managed well enough with a hero and heroine made out of clay.

Josephine thought the comparison was not apt. The Almighty had not had a troupe of unruly players to contend with and had not had to pay for the clay.

Fortunately, Lord York was taking care of things like that. The outstanding bills had been paid in the space of a week. She was not sure how but she was ever more grateful to him, and her fond feelings for him grew fonder.

However, there was nothing particularly romantic about their hours at the theater. There was simply too much to do. They were together nearly every day, beginning rehearsals before noon and working late into the evening. Such constant proximity brought back much of the happy ease of their childhood days together in Richmond, though Jo was not an onlooker now. The players and crew were as likely to turn to her as to Terence or Daniel when a decision had to be made.

Dear Daniel. There seemed to be nothing he would not do for her brother or for her. He seemed to watch over them both. But he had not kissed her again. They were never alone, of course. Yet she caught him watching her often enough. There was a fond look in his eyes each time, which warmed her through and through. He was wont to ask her advice on little things and not a few of the larger ones. She was pleased by his attention, very pleased indeed.

But Jo wondered just how and when they might find themselves away from all the others once more.

She wandered down another path, letting the large and somewhat cumbersome bag in her hand swing a little, determined to enjoy the outing for as long as she could.

She and Ginny had been left at the garden by the coachman several hours ago and he had only just returned. She looked over her shoulder to see him jump down with a leathern bucket in his hand

and look about for a pump to water the horses. He did not seem to have noticed her.

Not eager to leave, Jo kept to the path. She could see Ginny as well, on the other side of the garden, bending over the beds of herbs, sniffing at a flowering plant now and then, and crushing a leaf from another in her fingers.

The quiet paths hummed with bees and the air was filled with the mingled fragrance of early summer flowers. The sweetness, the realness of everything she saw refreshed her soul. She had been too long away from the country, and too confined at the theater. When she had stepped down from the carriage that morning, the sunlight had made her blink.

Jo came to a bench set beneath a trellis covered with rambling roses and sat down. With a smile, she opened her bag and took out the "wee present" that the ever-industrious McNeel had made just for her.

It was a desk, not exactly wee, but not very large and most ingeniously constructed, with a hinged lid that slanted and several interior compartments. She settled it upon her lap and lifted the lid.

Her mother's last letter was inside. Jo had been remiss in not answering it promptly. She unfolded it and read it again from start to finish.

Dearest Jo,

We are enjoying Bath, as much as we are able, taking the waters and seeing the sights. (The waters taste dreadful, by the way.) Your cousin Penelope assures me of the beneficial effects and my new physician says that I shall soon be skipping about like a lamb, but I do not know about that.

Speaking of lambs, your brother, who was so good as to write (and I am sure that I have you to thank

*for that) said that he is producing a play called The
Shepherdess. He assures me that the most scrupu-
lously moral persons would find nothing shocking
in it. He said the songs are wonderfully melodious
and that the most venerable theatergoers will be able
to sleep though them in perfect comfort. He also mentioned a chorus of nymphs and satyrs. It sounds
lovely, Jo!*

Josephine smiled. She could not imagine what
her mother would think of loudmouthed Molly, or
the rest of the scantily clad chorus.

*I am happy to know that his expensive educa-
tion serves him so well. Your brother took prizes in
Latin and Greek at Oxford, as you know (mater-
nal pride forces me to mention that once more—we
were so proud of him).*

Her mother had squeezed another sentence
above her parenthetical comment.

I am just as proud of you, my dear.

Jo smiled and read on.

*No doubt he has taught the nymphs and the
satyrs a bit of both. The performance will be most
educational.*

The nymphs and satyrs did not even speak the
King's English. But her parents need never know.
They did not come up to London as a rule.

*Your dear papa might even enjoy it! He has
found a friend, another retired vicar, with whom he
can discuss tricky theological questions and other*

*such matters. Mr. Shy does enjoy a churchy chin-wag
and they talk long into the night. I find the sound
of it quite soothing but the sense of it is lost upon
me. So I nap.*

Ah, yes. Her father was determined to find out
the meaning of it all. Simply enjoying life had apparently never occurred to him. Jo turned to the
second page.

*Yet I too have a new friend, a Mrs. Carp, an aged
widow who enjoys a quiet game of cards. We do not
gamble, of course. Your father would not approve.
He has visited Mrs. Carp only once. Her cat sicked
up a prodigious hairball upon his best overcoat and
it has never been the same. I mean the overcoat—
the cat is in good health. A hairball is a terrible
thing.*

Indeed, Jo mused. Her mother sounded happy
enough.

*And now I return to the subject of Penelope. She
has met a young scholar, a lover of antiquities, like
herself. They decipher hieroglyphics together far into
the night and use up all the oil in the lamp. It
seems to me that hieroglyphics would be difficult to
read with only moonbeams for illumination, yet
Penelope assures me that it can be done. Her young
scholar wears thick spectacles for his weak eyes and
prefers to work by moonlight, apparently.*

A skilled fortune hunter would, Jo thought. Her
plain but very rich cousin was clearly in danger of
being swept off her feet, bundled into a carriage,
and put on the road to Gretna Green.
But there was nothing Jo could do about it. She

felt the tiniest pang of guilt for giving Penelope those romance novels long ago. A seed had been planted. A sprout had shot up. A topiary of desire had grown tall.

Jo realized that she was beginning to think like Hugh Newsome, in silly symbols. Indeed, she thought with a smile, perhaps the greatest danger to be encountered in the theater was not to her morals but her mind, which she was likely to lose.

She folded up her mother's letter and put it away, taking out fresh paper to write a reply. She uncapped the ink bottle and put it into the hole that McNeel had fashioned to hold it. It fit perfectly and would not spill. Jo thought a moment and then began.

> *My dear Mama,*
> *I was happy indeed to receive your letter and to hear that you are enjoying Bath. Papa's new friend sounds most interesting and I am glad that you have found one as well. Do not overexert yourself, my dear Mama.*
> *We continue as before. Terence, of course, is busy at the theater as he explained in his letter to you. He has little time to spend with his sister.*

As the afternoon shadows grew a little longer, Jo filled several pages in a similarly vague way. She looked up, startled, when a very long shadow, a rather broad-shouldered one, fell across the paper.

"Lord York! Where have you come from?" She set the little desk and her writing things to one side, noting with secret pleasure that he had left off his coat and wore a plain shirt of white lawn, open at the collar. It revealed his neck, and a very nice neck it was, shown to advantage against the whiteness of the shirt.

His breeches, however, were streaked with dirt and the toes of his boots were uncharacteristically muddy.

"The coachman brought me. I did spy you here when I arrived but since you were writing, I decided not to bother you—well, not right away—and went walking by the river, where I slipped and fell."

"I hope you did not injure yourself."

"My pride was hurt but not badly. How pretty you look in this bower of roses."

How sweet of him to say so. Jo looked about for Ginny. There she was, in a nearby lane. They would have to behave. "Thank you, my lord. You look . . . like you used to. Muddy."

"I think that is a compliment but I am not sure. Yet I see approval in your eyes."

"Yes," she said. "You and Terence often got muddier than that when you hunted frogs. I used to watch you with utmost admiration." She had to admit it. She had not forgotten how it felt to be so much younger, waiting upon the bank at her nurse-maid's side, delighted by the daring of the big boys.

"Do you remember that?" He seemed quite pleased.

"Yes, of course."

"And do you remember the great frog we never could catch, the one we called Gus?"

"I never knew why he had that name." Such things loomed large in the memories of men. Lord York had mentioned the frog to Terence during their first meeting at the theater, when she had listened at the closed door. But she saw no need to tell him that she done that.

"His full name was the Great Uncatchable Sir Slippery. As in G.U.S.S. or simply Gus."

"Ah, of course!" She laughed.

"Do you suppose old Gus still lives under the bridge?"

"I do not know, Lord York. I have never looked, certainly. Proper young ladies do not roll up their drawers and pick up their dresses and go wading in rivers."

"You would, given half a chance."

She only smiled in reply.

He sat down beside her on the bench. "Can you not call me Daniel? No one is near."

She could guess what he had in mind. The great moment of her second kiss—no, her third—was at hand . . . but they were far from alone. "Ginny is close by," she said with prim regret.

He half-turned to see the wardrobe mistress on the next path and sighed.

"She seems to be enjoying herself. This is a pleasant place. I cannot tell you how glad I am to be here. I have had quite enough of the theater for today. Molly and Lizzie got into a fight. The screaming was dreadful."

"What do they have to fight about? They are not even in the same scenes."

"No, but they like the same man."

Jo's eyes opened wide. "Molly did not set her cap at Harry Longwood, did she?"

Lord York nodded. "She did, but Lizzie was the victor on the battlefield of love. And Harry knows which side his bread is buttered on. He will not stray. Besides, our trembling virgin slapped Molly hard enough to knock a wig off. Fortunately, she was not wearing one."

"Then what?"

"Molly slunk off through the wings, muttering imprecations."

"Oh, dear. I suppose I should not have left."

He slid an arm along the back of the bench. Jo did not move away.

"My dear Jo, you needed to get out. You have helped Lizzie rehearse her songs for *The Shepherdess* for hours each day. She knows every word and every note by now and so do you. And it is not as if you are going to sing them."

"Of course not." But Jo could not help wondering what he would do or say if some mischance kept Lizzie from going on. Of course, it would never happen. Lizzie would go on with two broken legs and a black eye, if it came to that.

But Jo knew, as did everyone else at the theater, that she was Lizzie's understudy, for the star of their show would have no other, whether Lord York liked it or not. But there were far greater sins than singing and playacting, surely.

Perhaps Lord York thought differently. He kept his distance from the performers, though he treated them with a measure of courtesy. Their outsized personalities and their talent for artifice seemed to make him uneasy.

It was a good thing he had not seen *her* that first day when he and Terence had come to visit Lizzie in her dressing room, forcing painted and powdered Jo to hide in the closet.

It had been a narrow escape, and once was enough. She had enjoyed looking so very different for a little while, but the stuff had proved dreadfully itchy and she had been afraid of breaking out in a rash. Fortunately she had not, but she also had not experimented with stage makeup since.

Daniel seemed to like her exactly as she was. Even late at night in the theater, after long hours of rehearsal had made her look weary, wrinkled her dress, and caused her hair to straggle, he still looked at her with tenderness—the way he was looking at her now. She blushed a bit and smoothed her skirts.

"I . . . I am glad to be here as well. It is a lovely place to write. And thank you for the use of the carriage. Ginny said she felt quite grand."

"Good. I think the world of Mrs. Goodchurch."

That was true. The motherly wardrobe mistress was the only person at the theater with whom Lord York seemed to feel comfortable, besides Jo and her brother.

"She is a very kind woman."

"And able to keep Lizzie in line as well. Perhaps that was why the battle over Harry began—Ginny was here."

"At your invitation. The fight was not her fault."

"Of course not. But let us talk of more pleasant things, Jo. What were you writing?"

She looked down at the desk at her side. "A letter to my mother."

"Give her my fond regards. Tell her that I remember her toasted cheese sandwiches and ask her for the recipe while you are at it."

"Cheese. Bread. Butter."

"There must be more to it than that."

"I will ask her." Jo picked up the desk, dipped her pen in the ink and scribbled another line or two. She waved the letter about in the air to dry it.

"By the way, that is a very nice little desk. Where did you buy it?"

"Mr. McNeel made it especially for me."

"Hmmm."

She cast an appraising glance at him. "That was a jealous sort of *hmmm*."

"What? You cannot read so much into one little word. And I am not jealous. It never occurred to me that you would consort with a carpenter."

"I beg your pardon?"

"Ah . . ." Lord York could not quite see how to extricate himself from this odd turn in the conversation. Perhaps it would be safest to stick to the subject of grammar. "My dear Jo, *hmmm* is not even a word, as far as I know."

"It is an interjection, I believe, and an interjection is a word."

He smiled at her and Josephine nearly melted. It was not the heat of the summer sun that did the trick but the warmth in his eyes. Oh, dear. She *had* spent too many long days in the theater—and memorized too many love songs.

"How does it open?" he asked, looking at the little desk.

She was happy to demonstrate and slipped her reply into the compartment inside, along with her writing things.

"And how does it close?"

She demonstrated that as well.

"Good. Now put it away and walk with me."

"You are in a commanding mood all of a sudden."

"Forgive me. But walk with me."

"Yes, Daniel."

He beamed and offered her his arm. Jo rose to take it, leaving the desk on the bench. They chose a winding path to nowhere in particular, and waved to Ginny, who straightened up to wave back.

"I often imagined us like this, Jo, walking down the lanes of Richmond."

"Did you?"

He nodded.

"Well, why did you imagine us walking about?" Really, he seemed to require considerable prodding to say what she wanted to hear. Which was not the same as him wanting to say it.

"Because I admired you. From afar."

How annoying, she thought. Not the admiration part. The afar part.

"But family matters took so much of my time then. And I never seemed to see you when I was not on my way to London to attend to our estate business or some such thing. I was forever rushing about. But you were always on my mind, Jo."

That is better, she thought.

"The years seemed to go by so quickly. I saw Terence in London, of course, but not as often as I would have liked. When he explained that he had bought the theater patent and suggested I purchase shares in it, I jumped at the chance."

"Like the Great Uncatchable Sir Slippery."

He laughed. "Yes. Long live old Gus."

"We really should go back to Richmond and see if he is still there, Daniel."

Lord York patted her arm. "Whenever you like. Your every wish is my command."

Better still, she thought with delight.

"I was thinking of inviting you and Terence and Ginny—and perhaps even Miss Loudermilk, though I draw the line at Harry—to Derrydale. For a week. Maybe two."

"What about the show?"

"Damn the show. Summer is coming. London will soon become disgustingly hot and smelly."

"I suppose Terence can spare me. But I do not know if he can do without his leading lady, and Lizzie can't do without Ginny."

"That is up to them. We shall have musicales and all the fun we want to, just like old times. Would you enjoy that, Jo?"

Best of all.

"Jo?"

"Oh!" she said, startled. "Yes, very much."

"Do you remember the house?"

"Yes, I do. Has it changed at all?"

"Very little. My brother had the house in Mayfair redecorated according to fashion. But he does not like Derrydale and has not been there since he came into the title. No, he leaves it to me to see to its upkeep."

They walked on to the end of the path and turned around again. The shadows were much longer and had taken on a twilight hue. The sun was about to dip below the horizon. Lord York nodded to Ginny as they approached her once more.

"Mrs. Goodchurch, are you ready to depart?"

"Yes. It has been a rare treat to come out. I thank ye, sir. Jo, where are your things?"

"On the bench, Ginny."

"I shall fetch them. Walk on, do."

If the wardrobe mistress thought anything of Jo and Daniel walking arm in arm, her peaceful countenance did not betray it. But Jo did not see the wink Ginny exchanged with Lord York when she wasn't looking.

Chapter Ten

Meanwhile, back at the theater, things had gone from bad to worse as the day wore on. After the catfight with Lizzie, Molly simply disappeared. She missed the first run-through for *The Castaway*.

Tom Higgins thought it was a bit of luck that Mr. Shy had left early for once, and that his sister and Lord York were not in the theater. Hugh Newsome had stood in for Molly at the run-through, imitating a bird swooping about, since no one else would, and looking altogether silly. Certainly she was the only one willing to be hoisted on a wire.

The castaway, Andy, had sung his songs well enough, with a little prompting in spots from another member of the cast. There was no one else in the scene besides him and Molly, so it had been left to Hugh and Andy to get through it, to scattered applause from the few players who had nothing else to do but watch.

Suddenly a burly young stagehand came barreling down the corridor, shouting for Tom. "We found her!"

"Hush, lad, no need to wake the dead. Not until opening night anyway. Where?"

"In McNeel's workshop."

"But we looked there, lad, twice."

The stagehand gasped for breath. "She was hiding."

"I tell ye, we looked!"

"She and Signor Arlecchino 'ave a bed behind the backdrops 'e was painting."

It was only a minute before Tom Higgins pushed the canvas aside and scowled at the happy, sleepy couple lying entwined in each other's arms. The burly stagehand craned his neck to see what he could.

"And what d'ye think ye're doing, Molly?"

"Having fun, Tom." She laughed and patted Arlecchino's unshaven face. "I love an Eyetalian man now and then. Very lusty they are. Isn't that right, ducks?" She kissed Arlecchino on the nose.

"*Si,*" he murmured. "I am ducks. We have the fun."

"Get up, both of ye!"

"He is up. You know what they say . . . Arly to bed, Arly to rise." Molly laughed raucously.

"Shut yer gob, girl!"

Hugh Newsome appeared at Tom's side. "I am sure there is some reasonable explanation. Do not yell at her, Tom. She is the only bird we have at the moment and there is no time to train another."

Arlecchino yawned. "What to explain? She has much beauty. Her front is like . . . like the pumpkins."

"I understand," Hugh said, a little irritably, "but Molly must come to rehearsal, Signor Arlecchino."

The Italian ignored him. "Not now. My love for her is very large. We sleep again."

"*Basta!*" Hugh said. "Enough!"

Signor Arlecchino seemed astonished to hear a word in his native tongue, however rudely spoken. "*Si, si,*" he muttered and was quiet.

Molly threw the covers over his head. "Poor little Arly. Be nice to him, Hughie. And ye'd better be nice to me, Tom. There *is* only one bird and I am it. Now, good night." She burrowed under the blankets.

A sound of muffled giggling ensued, followed by enthusiastic writhing.

"Cor," the stagehand said, a note of admiration in his voice. "She's right saucy. Loves to be loved. Wish I was next." He puffed up his chest and thumped it. "She needs an Englishman."

"Bugger off!" Tom cuffed him.

"Ow!"

"Thanks fer finding her, though." Tom pulled the canvas backdrop back to where it had been and left the lovers alone.

Terence got the story the next day from Tom. He listened to every detail, frowning. "Molly has us over a barrel. She can do as she pleases. She is quite right—we cannot replace her at this point."

"Naow, sir, we can't. But we don't have to put up with that Arlecchino scurrying about and speakin' his strange lingo. Have ye ever noticed how he is right there when there is trouble?"

"Name me one aspect of this production that has been free of trouble, Tom. Arlecchino can't be everywhere at once."

"Seems like he is."

"If he makes Molly happy, then he stays."

"I take yer meaning. Like the blacksmith makes Lizzie happy, you mean."

Terence covered his face with his hands and

peered out through his fingers. "Oh, no. I hoped she would wait a little while."

"I happened to overhear—" Tom began.

"Yes, go on. That is what I pay you for, among other things: overhearing."

"But you haven't paid me. Anyway, Lizzie whispered somefink to Dora about what a fine man Longwood was and how she wasn't getting any younger while they were all waiting backstage."

"But that does not mean that she and the blacksmith are—"

"The sofa squeaks in her dressing room at odd hours, sir."

Terence rose from his desk and paced the carpet. "We could remove the sofa."

"You know how performers is, sir. Sneaky. Very sneaky. Especially when they are feelin' amorous. Any horizontal surface will do."

"I cannot argue the point. You have worked in the theater far longer than I have, Tom."

"Aye, sir."

Terence paused and took a deep breath. "I wonder who else will be struck by Cupid's arrow. Do you know, Tom, I have not been in love for the longest time myself. Perhaps I will be next."

"Well, I would not say Molly and Lizzie are in love, sir. They just want a bit of fun, is all."

"Then we must pretend that we don't notice. And do not breathe a word of this to Lord York. He thinks theater folk are immoral as it is. And he also thinks Jo should not spend so much time here. He had his coachman drive her and Ginny to the gardens of Chelsea yesterday."

"I know. I spoke wif him late in the afternoon. Just before he went in that fine carriage o' his to bring her home."

Terence raised an eyebrow. "He went? How very interesting. I did not know that he had met her there. Jo was asleep when I got home, and she said nothing of it at breakfast."

"I am sure our Miss Jo has done no wrong," Tom said nervously.

"Of course not. As far as I know, my sister has never even been kissed. Lord York seems to think of her as a friend. We all grew up together in Richmond, you know."

"Ye may have mentioned it, sir."

"I have tried my best to bring them together."

"Ye yelled at him to look into her eyes when we was testing the lights. That oughter have done the trick."

Terence picked up a bottle of madeira and poured himself a small glass. "I did not yell. I requested that he look into Jo's eyes. And he did. But the magic . . . didn't happen." He tossed the thick, sweet wine down his throat in one go and poured another glass. On second thought, he poured one for Tom as well. "Will you join me?"

"Yes, sir," the stage manager said with alacrity, taking the glass. He imitated Terence and swallowed all of it at once. "What magic would that be, sir?"

"The magic of love, theater style. A rosy glow in the air—lighting is very important, Tom—and a table for two. All make-believe but somehow very real. It didn't work, though." He gave Tom a sad look. "Shall we have another?"

"Certainly, sir. I am happy to be of assistance t'ye. Whenever ye need a bottle finished, call old Tom."

Terence poured and they drank.

"But Miss Jo is very young," Tom pointed out. "She will have many a suitor, mark my words."

"Of course," Terence said moodily. "But it would be so convenient if she and Lord York would hurry up and fall in love. I would rather not interview potential suitors for her. She is here and he is here . . . she likes him, he likes her. What more do they need?"

"Give them time, sir."

Terence poured another glass and sipped it. He had decided to slow down but not stop. "Time? Is that all? Well, it is free, even if we are running out of it. But this damned show takes all my time."

"Opening night is not far away, sir. Your first."

"Do not remind me," Terence said gloomily. "At least we are no longer running out of money, now that Daniel has taken over the books. I checked his entries and calculations, just for the practice. It seems to me that there is income, though we have sold no tickets as yet. Perhaps Daniel is covering our expenses from his own pocket. But I could be wrong. I have no head for such things."

"Yes, sir," Tom said amiably. "Pass the bottle, if you would."

The madeira changed hands briefly and ended up on Terence's desk. He poured himself another and set it down unsteadily, but managed to right it just before it spilled.

"Do you know, Tom, I had hoped to make money in the theater." Terence laughed. "What a joke, eh?" He put his feet up on top of a pile of ledgers and slid down into his chair.

Tom grinned and gulped his wine. "There are straighter paths to the poorhouse, sir."

"Well said."

The stage manager settled himself in the large armchair and put his feet up on the seat of a smaller one. "It is a risky business and no mistake."

"What I need, Tommy boy, is an heiress."

Tom took another gulp. "Can't help ye with that. Don't know any."

"I have courted several. Most assiduously."

"What happened?"

Terence leaned back in his chair. "They would not have me. Heiresses are a bit skittish, Tommy. They prefer tame fellows, and I am not like that."

Tom thought it over. "Ye could pretend t'be tame for as long as it took to get one to marry ye."

"Ah, but the feminine mind is subtle. Even an inexperienced heiress would see through a ruse like that. They tend to be educated, though a few are too silly and nothing sticks."

"Have ye looked for a silly girl, sir?"

"Of course. And I found one. But her papa was extra-vigilant and she had five older brothers."

"Ye might've been horsewhipped," Tom murmured. "Young fellows is hotblooded when it comes to defendin' the family honor."

"They advised me to cease and desist my attentions to their sister in no uncertain terms."

"What did ye do?"

"I flicked a glove at them, picked up my hat, and left their house at once."

The stage manager gave him an admiring look. "Ye do live dangerously, sir. I have never flicked a glove at no one nor faced a gang of horsewhippers. No, I flirt with barmaids."

"That has its advantages," Terence said.

"Aye, free ale." Tom grinned and let his head loll back. "And my Jill don't seem to mind if I don't come home every night. I expect she has a stage-hand on the side herself."

"Ah, yes, your Jill. The wardrobe mistress at Drury Lane and our part-time spy. She has not been a fountain of information lately. Perhaps you ought to let the barmaids alone."

"Jill don't care about them. But she ain't been paid by you, neither."

Terence scowled and dug in his pockets. He handed Tom a few coins. "That is all I have. Please see that it gets to her."

"May I have the bottle of madeira into the bargain? Jill does like a drop of it now and then. Says it makes her ears warm. She likes the feeling."

"By all means."

Terence handed the madeira to Tom and began to pace upon the carpet. "Now, to return to the problem of heiresses. I need one, but not an ordinary one."

Tom swirled the thick wine in his glass and watched it trickle down the sides of the glass. "Can ye afford to be so particular, sir?"

"Let me explain. I need an heiress with something to hide. A shocking episode in her past, perhaps. An affair that ended badly, with someone else's outraged wife flinging crockery."

"Always a pity about the crockery. That sort o' fight gets expensive."

"Yes, Tom. I myself once had a turkey platter cracked over my head."

"By someone else's wife?"

"No. Never mind the details. The doctor's bill was exorbitant."

"That there exorbitant sounds like a bad business, sir."

"Indeed it is."

Tom grew thoughtful. "You could advertise— no, no, that won't do. Heiresses don't answer 'em. Wouldn't be proper. And they wouldn't place a notice themselves, because of the need to hide from them outraged wives and vigilant papas. You could look for advertisements for crockery menders. They might know a naughty heiress."

Terence sighed. "You think things through, Tommy. I like that about you."

"Thank'ee kindly, sir."

"There must be a way to find the woman of my mercenary dreams."

"Ask yer sister to help. She goes to the mercer's every day for thread and such."

"Mercenary means moneygrubbing, Tommy. It has nothing to do with thread. I cannot ask Jo. She still believes in love and sees nothing romantic in marrying for money."

A long silence fell.

"She is a good girl with a good heart, sir. We is all very fond of her."

"As am I," Terence said.

"She will understand, Mr. Shy. She has learned a lot about life in this here theater."

Terence ceased his pacing and looked at Tom. "What has she learned?"

The stage manager hemmed and hawed. "Well, I don't know exactly. Perhaps that things ain't what they seem sometimes. That is a useful thing to know."

"But a sad one." Terence's expression grew wistful. "I never should have brought her here. She was so innocent—"

"She still is, Mr. Shy, mark my words."

"I didn't mean *that*, Tommy. I was only feeling maudlin. Pass the wine. I will become loud and sentimental next. I might even weep."

Tom clutched the bottle. "Ye said my Jill could have it!"

"So I did," Terence said irritably. He strode back to the desk and pulled out an unopened bottle from a dark recess. "This is the last of it. But in return Jill has to provide current information on the Drury Lane production. We must outdo them if we are to make a profit."

"Have ye given up hunting an heiress, then?"

Terence grinned at him. "Hmmm . . . *Hunting the Heiress*. What a wonderful title for a play. I will suggest it to Hugh."

"Tell him I came it up wif it."

"Of course. He will be very pleased. But I will tell him nothing else of what we said."

"It were extremely confidential."

"Yes, and you must not repeat a word to anyone. I was merely . . . thinking aloud and making cynical jokes. I would not marry just for money, you know."

"Course not. You were a little drunk."

"Yes."

"My lips is sealed, sir. Just as soon as I finish what's left in the bottle."

Terence waved a hand. "Drink up. Wine, women, and song are life's great diversions."

"I wish you luck with finding the right woman, sir," Tom said, draining the dregs of the wine and coughing. "One with plenty of mercenary."

"Thank you, Tommy. I will take that empty bottle, if you don't mind. Wouldn't want Lord York to think the worst."

"No, sir." Tom exchanged the one in his hand for the unopened bottle Terence held.

"Give Jill my regards. And don't worry about me, Tom. An heiress would be an easy way out of my financial difficulties, but I am no more likely to find one than our singing castaway upon his lonely rock."

Tom got to his feet and swayed. "You missed his rehearsal. He sang well, even if Molly wasn't there."

"Good. This ridiculous production is coming together slowly but surely. Bit of a hodgepodge, to be sure, with so many acts, but it has tremendous potential. I would even dare to call it good. In spots."

"Don't say that, sir."

"But it *is* good. It will be better. It might even be a hit."

"Shh! Ye mustn't say things like that!"

"Why not, Tom?"

The stage manager's expression collapsed into worried wrinkles. "It's bad luck."

"Oh, surely you don't believe that superstitious nonsense."

Tom scowled. "I do believe it. Brace yerself, sir. The worst is yet to come." He clasped the unopened bottle of madeira to his chest and left without a backward glance.

Terence looked after him, shaking his head.

The golden light of afternoon streamed through the tall windows of the library in the Mayfair house. Daniel sat in the armchair by the fireplace, just as he had upon the night when he first contemplated the courtship of Jo. But he sat a little straighter, well pleased with himself, and he sipped from a glass of wine.

The latest wrinkle—getting her away from the theater and the watchful, gossipy players—had been a stroke of genius. Ginny had helped with that business about needing lavender, of course.

Their interlude, however brief, had been sweet. Dear Jo. She had looked so pretty under the trellis of rambling roses. Daniel had been ready to kiss her then and there. But Ginny had been too close and Jo had seen her. She was an intelligent girl and would have realized instantly that the whole thing had been planned if she'd seen Ginny scurry off.

No, the wardrobe mistress had played her part well. Jo had not suspected a thing.

His invitation to Derrydale had been accepted. He'd had to invite a few others, for the sake of decency. Daniel remembered Jo quoting Lizzie on the subject—*decency be damned*—and smiled to himself.

He was more determined than ever to observe every propriety, though Jo sometimes twitted him for being a stuffed shirt. Terence, eccentric as always, simply did not seem to care about his sister's reputation. But Daniel did. For all that Jo kept company with theater folk, she was not of the theater nor was she a performer. She might find them amusing, but then, she was young.

It crossed his mind that he was not that old, and theater folk *were* amusing. Very amusing. He had even begun to like Lizzie Loudermilk and her outrageous jokes at her own expense.

His parents would have been shocked, but his parents were no longer alive. Daniel looked up at the portrait of his mother over the fireplace. It was she who had taught him to love music and all the arts, for she had loved them as well. Like Jo, she had been a vicar's daughter, gently born but poor.

She had married his father before anyone knew he would come into the title. The eventual earl had lived in harmony with his young bride for years in a cottage very like The Elms, before his six older brothers succumbed one by one to the deleterious effects of heavy drinking, whoring, and consumption.

As far as Daniel was concerned, the great house upon the Derrydale estate still seemed to resonate with his mother's presence, though she had died when he was young. He looked forward to showing it to Jo again and wondered what, if anything, she remembered of her few visits there.

The earl had not remarried, and grew old too soon, distressed to see that his oldest son, Daniel's brother, Gerald, was more dissolute than the six bad uncles put together.

They were long dead. Their sins and sorrows were all water under the Richmond bridge by now.

Daniel raised his glass and toasted the uncles. Their portraits were much smaller—almost miniatures—and had been set upon a shelf in a neat row.

Perhaps, he thought, he had inherited a little of their wildness or else he would not enjoy the theater as he did.

He did not toast Gerald's portrait. His brother's smug face and bibulous nose already showed the signs of drinking to excess, even prettied up in oils by a society painter.

Daniel again turned his thoughts to Jo. The carriage ride home had gone exactly as planned, the happy culmination of their day away from the endless rehearsals.

He had sat to one side, with Ginny in the middle and Jo on the other side. But Ginny had asked to be let out first, at the small shop in the Strand where she shared an apartment with another woman.

And he had been alone with Jo at last.

She had immediately moved the bag with the portable desk between them, into the space that Ginny had vacated, and its corners had poked him in the thigh. He had not moved it, somewhat amused that she had used it as a barrier. It had not stopped him.

He had let one arm slide over the back of the seat and had drawn her to him. Jo had not resisted.

She had leaned over the desk and sought his lips, returning his kisses with tender passion.

That was all they had done. He had not permitted himself to go further.

Daniel took another sip of the mellow wine and wondered what she was doing now.

The postman had come to Guilford Street, slipping letters through the slots of each neatly painted door. There was only one for Jo. She recognized her mother's spidery hand at once. So their letters would cross, as often happened.

She ran upstairs to her bedroom, where she preferred to see to her correspondence, and rattled about in the drawer of her desk for a letter opener. She slid it under the wax seal, which came away from the paper with a faint pop.

Jo unfolded the missive and leaned back upon the bed to read. But the pillows were too plump and neat. She turned around to thrash them into a proper state of submission and finally settled down.

My dearest Jo,

So much has happened since I last wrote, I scarcely know where to begin. It seems that Penelope and her bespectacled scholar—whose name I will not mention, it is anathema to me—have gone too far.

Their moonlight meetings, supposedly to decipher Egyptian hieroglyphics, were a ruse. I must admit that I was fooled. Penelope has declared her eternal love for this persuasive snake in the grass, who has disappeared. No doubt he plans to elope with her. He is penniless, of course. Her fortune and her reputation are at grave risk. My dearest girl, I am ever so glad that you do not go in for clandestine kisses and that sort of thing!

Jo sat bolt upright upon the bed. She had just experienced that sort of thing—well, not the ultimate sort of thing . . . they had not done more than kiss—in Lord York's big black carriage. With the door closed.

> *Your father and I are bringing her to London at once on the next stage. Perhaps you can talk some sense into Penny. She will not listen to me or to him. She can share your room, to prevent midnight escapes, and we will sleep in the guest bedroom that Terence mentioned.*
>
> *It is a great advantage under the circumstances that you are always at home. Penny will have to be watched like a hawk day and night.*
> *Your loving Mama*
> *P.S. We can take turns.*

Jo's heart sank. She threw the letter upon the floor. There was no sense in writing back. By the time her response reached Bath, her parents and Penelope would already be in London.

The snake in the grass would follow, no doubt.

She wondered who he was and what he looked like. Her mother had offered no particulars. If they were to protect Penny, Jo would have to have this vital information.

Not that she wanted it.

She would be unable to go to the theater. She would have to stay home and hover over Penny. Lord York might visit at Guilford Street, because her parents knew him, but she would not be able to ride in his carriage, or dawdle the afternoon away, laughing with Lizzie and Ginny in the dressing rooms, or watch rehearsals, or help Mr. McNeel build and paint.

Nooooooooooo. She would have to be perfectly

respectable and set an example for her wayward cousin, who had always been perfectly respectable herself until the appearance of the snake.

Jo might even miss opening night.

She flung herself back into the pillows and closed her eyes. She was too angry to cry.

Chapter Eleven

Two days later at Guilford Street . . .

Dinner was a grim affair. Penelope refused to eat, wiping her tears away with a drenched, twisted handkerchief, looking utterly miserable and faintly sick.

Jo waved to the maid to clear the table. Penelope rose. They all rose with her.

"I do not plan to throw myself out the dining room window, if that is what you are all worried about. You do not have to watch my every move, you know."

Mrs. Shy coughed discreetly and cast a look at the wide-eyed maid. "Let us discuss this in the drawing room, if you please, Penny."

Jo's plain cousin let out a lugubrious sigh. If only Penny would not carry on like the heroine of a bad opera, Jo thought with some annoyance. After all, she had done nothing but exchange kisses with a man under the moonlight. Jo had done the same. The situation was not all that dire.

"My dear aunt," Penelope began, composing herself. "We have endured two days in each other's company, crowded inside the stagecoach from Bath. I daresay you and Uncle found it quite trying."

"My health is not the best, my girl," Mrs. Shy said crisply.

"You must rest," her husband said to her. He glared at Penelope.

She cast down her eyes. "I am dreadfully sorry for the trouble I have caused. But I must talk to Jo . . . alone."

"Very well. I am exhausted." Mrs. Shy threw down her serviette and left the dining room, trailed by the vicar.

Jo looked after them with surprise. "Really, Penelope, how could you be so foolish? Such a brouhaha over a few kisses."

"Let me explain," Penelope begged, "but not here."

Jo took her cousin's arm and walked with her to the drawing room, not saying another word. She settled herself in one armchair and indicated that Penelope should take the other.

"Please do explain. I am ready to listen."

"You must promise not to tell your mother everything, Jo."

"All right," Jo said slowly, wondering what revelations lay in store.

"Oliver has disappeared."

"That does not surprise me. Well, it does a little. My mother seemed to think he was after your inheritance. Money exerts a powerful magnetic force, you know. She expected him to follow you to London."

"He did not. I never told him of it, and it is not as if I wear fashionable clothes or jewels. How would he have known? Your mama would never dream of mentioning my money."

Jo nodded. "Were you two really engaged in the study of hieroglyphics?"

"I was teaching him. He pretended to learn."

"How romantic."

"It was to me," Penelope said wistfully. "One wants to share what one loves with one's lover."

"I have lost track of the ones. But never mind. You and Oliver were—was he a scholar?"

"No, but he looked ever so handsome in spectacles."

Jo sighed. "Penelope, you have had the benefit of an excellent education. Surely you know that looks are deceiving."

Penelope wiped a tear. "Perhaps I was willing to be deceived. Jo, imagine my situation. There I was in Bath, accompanying my elderly aunt and uncle to the Pump Room and other smelly places filled with complaining invalids.

"Yes, I wanted to go and I am very fond of your mother. But I felt . . . almost invisible. Not one man looked at me. Not really. A few looked through me, if you know what I mean."

Jo raised an eyebrow but she let her cousin talk.

"It is not easy to be plain and a little plump, you know," Penelope went on. "An excellent education is all very well but what use it will ever be to me, I do not know. No one wants to dally with a bluestocking."

"Perhaps not," Jo agreed.

"And is there something wrong with wanting something more? Oliver was kind to me. Oliver was interested in my work. Oliver danced with me. Oliver kissed me."

"And now Oliver is gone. But the world continues to spin. You will get over him."

Penelope rose to walk about the drawing room in an agitated way. Jo could see that her cousin was perhaps a bit plumper than the last time they had met and as ungainly as always. She did feel sorry for Penny. She just felt sorrier for herself.

Jo had to pretend she actually enjoyed humdrum domesticity for as long as her parents chose to stay at the Guilford Street house. It was not indefinite, of course, but still . . . it was an awful nuisance.

She had dashed off a note to Lord York, explaining the matter in a few brief words. At least he knew her parents. He would be sure to call at the house as soon as he could and had been instructed to behave with exemplary restraint.

She could not tell her dear mama of her tender feelings for Daniel, or any of the rest of it.

Especially not since Penelope had been caught kissing—oh, dreadful deed!—a fortune hunter, posing as a scholar in prop spectacles. But apparently Oliver had not even been a real fortune hunter, only an ordinary bounder. Her cousin's misadventure had a whiff of farce about it. But Penny's misery seemed all too real.

"Penny, did you truly know nothing of love?"

"Nothing."

"Oh, dear. But it seems to me that you are too intelligent to be so distraught over losing a false lover. He kissed you and he danced with you. But your little affair, if I may call it that, clearly meant much more to you than it did to him and that is unfortunate."

Penny swallowed hard. "Do you remember the romance novels that you gave me, Jo?"

"Yes. You said you did not see what all the fuss was about."

"Now I know," she said sadly.

"But those books are fiction. You were taught to value facts."

Penelope wrung her hands. "To hell with facts. I

never learned about heroes or villains or how to know if love is real or what a woman scorned should do. They do seem to survive in books, as a rule."

"Well, yes," Jo agreed. "If the heroine throws herself off a cliff on page two, there will have to be a lot of talking at her funeral, pages and pages of it, to fill up the rest."

"Yes," Penny said, "that is what I am getting at. She must tumble down and crawl back up the rocks, and struggle. And her hero will be waiting."

Jo was quiet for a moment. "You don't expect that Oliver is waiting for you, do you?"

"No." Penelope looked at her with stricken eyes and sat down in the armchair again.

"Penny, what really happened? Why are you so upset?"

"He . . . he did more than kiss me, Jo. I have missed my courses for two months. There is nothing I can do about it. I am going to have a baby."

"Oh!" Jo was thunderstruck. "Does my mother know that?"

"No, and you promised not to tell her."

"I would never. Oh, my poor Penny! I had no idea! But I will help you, however I can." She embraced her friend, now in a full flood of tears.

"You are very kind, Jo. Most would not. But I will not abandon my baby to a wet nurse or leave it at the Foundling Hospital. I might . . . go away somewhere. I have enough money to live wherever I want to. I could go to Egypt."

"Of course," Jo said, patting Penny's tear-streaked cheek and crying a little herself. "Why didn't I think of that? You and your innocent babe will ride off into the sunset upon a camel, wrapped in yashmaks or whatever it is they wear."

"Djellabas, I believe. It is a sort of loose robe. The yashmak is a scarf."

"Penny, dear, you cannot go to Egypt. Please don't talk nonsense. There is a way out of every difficulty."

Penelope wiped her eyes. "Not this one."

"Perhaps I can help," said a masculine voice.

Jo looked up. "Terence! How much did you hear?"

Terence walked into the room. "Something about a camel. And a djellaba. What is going on? Mama and Papa have retired for the night after arriving quite unexpectedly from Bath—you never did tell why they were coming, Jo—and now I find two weeping women in the drawing room. May I venture a guess that all is not quite right with the world?"

"Oh, the world will continue to spin. Jo says so." Penelope sniffed back her tears.

"Jo is always right, you know," Terence said breezily.

A few hours later . . .

Jo made Penny comfortable in her own room and tiptoed down the stairs. Terence was waiting for her in the drawing room, she knew. She opened the door quietly to see him sitting by the lamp, a glass of brandy in his hand.

"What was that all about? I have never seen Penelope so emotional."

"Oh, nothing. A broken heart. She will get over it."

"Is that why Mama and Papa brought her back from Bath?"

"Yes."

"How long are they all staying?"

"Until . . . I don't know, Terence. I expect that our parents will want to return to The Elms as soon as possible, but they want me to stay here with Penny and keep her from running away with a fortune-hunting blackguard."

"Who? Is he here? I seem to have missed the second act."

"He has disappeared. And he is not really a fortune hunter. Apparently he did not even know that Penelope was an heiress. They were studying hieroglyphics together and one thing led to another—"

"Damned hieroglyphics," Terence said affably. "There you are, looking at cartouches of jackals and ibises and crocodiles, and before you know it, someone is nuzzling your ear. Happens to me all the time."

Jo did not know whether to laugh or cry. The lateness of the hour, Penelope's earth-shattering news, her own shock—everything had her on an emotional edge.

"It is good to see Penelope again. I have always liked her. Intelligent girl. Not a beauty but most enjoyable to talk to."

"Yes. Yes, she is." Jo had not known that her brother thought so highly of their cousin. Her heart rejoiced, then sank. She took a deep breath, remembering her mother's motto: *Always do the right thing, Jo. Your heart will tell you what that is.*

She was not at all sure that telling Terence of Penelope's predicament was the right thing to do. But she trusted her brother, despite his eccentricity, and time was of the essence.

"I am glad to hear that you like her. I was hoping you would—that is, if you felt so inclined—"

"Oh, stop hemming and hawing. Do you want me to escort her to a ball or something like that?"

"No, I was going to ask you to marry her."

"What?"

Chapter Twelve

"I mean a sham marriage, of course. A real divorce afterward would require an Act of Parliament and—"

"Have you lost your mind?" Terence rose and placed a hand on her forehead. "Are you suffering from a fever?"

Jo batted his hand away.

"Penelope needs our help."

"A few hours ago she seemed to be needing a camel. What the devil is going on?"

"I cannot tell you."

"You must."

Jo took a deep breath. "Penelope is going to have a baby."

"What? Whose?"

"It doesn't matter."

Terence, as was his wont, began to pace. "Well, it matters to me. She is my cousin, but it is not my baby, and I should like to know who done the deed. Oh . . ." He paused. "The student of hieroglyphics, was it?"

Jo nodded.

"So you think I should marry her."

"In a sham ceremony."

He threw up his hands. "There. You have been at the theater too long. I blame myself. You now believe that paper moons are real and that Molly can actually fly."

"Penelope's dilemma is very real."

"Yes, I suppose so. But that does not mean that I—do you know, Jo, not two days ago Tom Higgins and I were getting to the bottom of a rather good bottle of madeira. I said in jest that all our problems would be over if only I could marry an heiress with something to hide. And it seems that divine providence has dropped one in my lap."

"Think of it as a sign."

"But what does it mean?" Terence shook his head. "It seems incredible. Penelope with child? And unwed? She was always such a serious girl."

"Yes, and she still is."

Her brother looked at her levelly. "This wild idea is all yours, I take it."

"Yes."

He began to pace again. "Have you ever wondered why you and I are so unlike our parents? They are deeply moral people, upright, blameless in every way, eminently sensible—"

"Perhaps we were left upon their doorstep by fairies."

Terence snapped his fingers. "That's it! I knew there was a rational answer."

"Oh, Terence. It does not matter if we are not like Mama and Papa in every respect. We are no less moral than they are, but we are . . . oh, what is the word?

"Less conventional."

"Yes, that is it exactly. Perhaps living in London has changed us, or—well, as you say, perhaps it is the theater. But surely helping Penelope is the right thing to do."

Jo allowed her brother to lead her to a chair and settle her into it.

"Helping Penelope is one thing," he said. "Marrying her is quite another. You are overwrought and overtired. But there is a lesson to be learned here. Kisses have consequences."

She burst into tears.

"Jo! Whatever is the matter now?"

She found the sodden handkershief that Penelope had left behind and bawled into it.

"You are not . . . you cannot be . . . has Daniel? No, he would never—dear God, girl! Explain yourself!"

"It is not what you think! He has kissed me. I let him. I liked it. But that is all."

"Then why are you crying, Jo?"

She gulped. "I don't know. I was so shocked by Penelope's news, and so afraid for her. And I still am. I could not think what to do and said the first thing that came into my head. I need a rest. Do you know, Daniel invited Ginny and Lizzie and me to Derrydale."

Terence nodded and stroked her hair. "You must go."

"What about Penelope?"

"She can go with you. Send him a note and say that your cousin has arrived unexpectedly. He will not mind. You will require a chaperone. I cannot spare Lizzie and Ginny for more than a few days in the midst of rehearsals."

Jo smiled wanly. "Chaperones are supposed to be elderly females of ironclad respectability, not unwed mothers. What will he say?"

"I daresay Penelope looks respectable enough. She was never one to follow the fashions. And she has told no one but you about her condition, is that correct?"

"Yes."

"Then he doesn't have to know. Go to Derrydale, and take Mama and Papa back to The Elms. I will carry on bravely by myself at the theater."

Jo patted his hand. "My hero."

He shrugged. "An unlikely one, to be sure. But perhaps I can find a way to help Penelope. Never fear."

"Derrydale–Richmond coach, leaving now," said Tom. "Drop yer luggage here, ladies. Ow! I didn't mean on my foot, Lizzie."

"Then get your foot out of my way."

He picked up her portmanteau. "Still haven't forgiven me for pullin' ye and Molly apart, I see."

"No, and I never will." The bosomy redhead swept by him regally.

"Suit yerself."

Tom tossed her luggage atop the rest. He was driving the wagon they used to transport large pieces of scenery, as the party had grown so large. There was just enough room for them in Lord York's black carriage but none for their things or the Shys's maid-of-all-work, who would ride with him.

Josephine, her parents, her cousin Penelope, Lizzie, Ginny, and Lord York himself milled about, seeing to last-minute preparations.

They clambered into the carriage one by one but Lizzie lingered upon the cobblestones until Harry Longwood came tearing out of the theater.

"Here is my blacksmith! He has hammered my heart upon the anvil of his love!"

"Oh, do shut up, Lizzie," said Ginny. "Yer nonsense quite gives me the headache."

The blacksmith bestowed a gentle kiss upon Lizzie's cheek.

"Thank you, my darling," she said, and got in last of all. Harry stood there disconsolately, tears in his eyes and sheet music in his hand, waving good-bye with it when the carriage rolled away toward the Strand.

They had been on the road for less than an hour when Mr. Shy began to snore. The day was warm and his elderly wife leaned against him and was soon fast asleep as well. Ginny, Lizzie, and Penelope jounced up and down, even though they were squeezed together on the backward-facing seat. Jo and Daniel, bracketing the Shys, offered polite smiles.

"I can't get comfy," Lizzie said.

"None of us can," Ginny replied. "Get used to it."

"Dear me, you would never know I am the star of a show. This carriage is not big enough."

"You are too big for it, Lizzie."

"Well, I never!" The singer settled back into outraged silence.

Ginny looked over at Penelope. "And how are ye faring, my dear?"

"Oh, very well," Penelope said a little weakly.

Josephine noticed that her cousin's face was pale. She looked as if she was about to be sick. "Open the window flap, Penny. You need some fresh air."

"We all do," Ginny said. "It is very nice of ye to invite us to the country, sir."

Lord York inclined his head. "I hope you will enjoy your stay, Mrs. Goodchurch."

"Nice manners he has," Lizzie commented, winking at Daniel. "That is the best part about lords. That, and the jewelry. You do get nice presents from a nobleman. But I was always more partial to a handsome fellow in livery. Do you remember the duke's footman, Ginny, the tall one who—"

"Lizzie," the wardrobe mistress said warningly, "not here." She pointed to the elderly couple.

"They are fast asleep, Ginny."

"That does not mean ye can say whatever ye wish. We have two proper young ladies with us as well. They do not need to hear ye talk about footmen."

"Oh, it won't hurt them."

But Lizzie said no more, and soon enough her eyelids fluttered closed. She leaned against Penelope's plump shoulder, opened her eyes halfway to see if anyone had noticed, and then fell asleep with her mouth open, somehow managing to remain upright.

Ginny's bright eyes flashed with merriment. "Who's next? Lord York? Our Jo?"

He sat up quite straight. "Not I."

"Lord York is too dignified for that," Jo said. "And I cannot sleep. I feel as if I have not been home for years. It is all so familiar and so dear."

"So ye don't miss London then, Jo?"

"No, not yet. But perhaps I will in time."

"How long did yer brother say ye could stay?"

"I must help my parents settle in, Ginny, and see that they have everything they need. And then Penelope and I will drive round our old haunts and look at the village shops. And Lord York and I plan to visit an old friend."

"Oh, very nice. Who?" Ginny inquired. "Not that I know anyone in Richmond. Seems dreadful far away to me, even though I know it's not. But then I am London–born and London–bred."

"His name is Gus. He is a very large frog who lives under the Richmond bridge."

"Visiting frogs? I like that." Ginny laughed. "Ye

are a country girl, Jo, and no mistake. Mind she does not fall in the water, Lord York. She might catch cold."

Lizzie's eyes opened suddenly. "Catch cold?" she said in a deep, dramatic voice. "Those are fatal words to a singer. Who has a cold?"

"No one, Lizzie. Go back to sleep."

The singer closed her eyes again.

Ginny cast a curious look at Penelope, who had not said a word but kept her face quite close to the open window, breathing deeply of the fresh country air. "Miss Penelope, are ye all right?"

"Yes," said Penelope, "quite all right. I was just looking at the sheep. There are so many."

"My neighbors use them to crop the grass in their parks. Nothing like flocks of sheep to do the job right. And they add a bucolic touch," Lord York explained.

"Cor," Ginny said, "imagine keeping sheep just to do the lawn."

"I have a small flock myself."

Jo remembered the vast expanse of green velvet lawn that swept down from the great house at Derrydale and felt a little uneasy. Daniel was a second son, to be sure, and worked for his living, but she sometimes forgot that he had grown up with all the trappings of wealth and power.

"How many?" she heard Ginny asking him.

"Six ewes and two lambs."

"That's very manageable, for a flock," said Ginny, as if she knew all about sheep. "Ye wouldn't want too many."

"No." Lord York smiled.

"How big are the lambs?" she asked.

"Big enough to make trouble. They might come over to investigate us when we arrive. Or they might be off with their mothers, grazing."

"Cor," Ginny said again, "yer own lambs. How nice. I should like a frisky little lamb."

"They grow up quickly, Mrs. Goodchurch."

"I expect ye're right."

The traveling party fell into a companionable silence as more miles passed by. Ginny exclaimed over the scenery; Jo kept an eye on Penelope; Penelope took deep breaths; and the Shys snored peacefully. Lizzie sat bolt upright with her eyes closed and her mouth open, looking like a magnificent, redheaded statue that was being transported to a new site.

Lord York gave Jo a warm look and a slight smile when he thought that no one would see. And before too long, they had arrived.

Jo helped Penelope down and climbed back in herself. The carriage would continue on to Richmond and leave the older Shys at The Elms.

"Be brave," she whispered in her cousin's ear.

"I shall." Penelope patted her hand.

Mrs. Shy waved good-bye, still seeming rather piqued at Penelope. Jo could hardly blame her. Mr. Shy slept on.

Tom Higgins pulled up behind them in the theater's wagon and began to unload the luggage. He took particular care to drop Lizzie's portmanteau on her foot when she came to claim it.

Ginny noticed and put a restraining hand on Lizzie's arm. "Now, now, ye are not in the theater. Behave."

Tom assisted the Shys's maid down to the ground and then helped her into the carriage. She sat next to old Mrs. Shy, looking timidly at the façade of the grand house.

"Our house is much smaller, Sarah," Jo said.

"Oh. Very good, miss. I cannot imagine cleaning such a big house as that."

"They have a housekeeper and many servants. No one person has to do it all."

"Yes, miss."

Once the Shys were ready, the coachman signaled the horses to go. And soon they were rolling back down the drive and over roads that Josephine knew well.

"How does it feel to be home, Jo?" her mother asked. The old lady covered a yawn, but she stayed awake.

"Oh, Mama, I feel as if I have been away for a hundred years, not just months. It is the oddest sensation."

"Well, the seasons changed while you were gone. I suppose that accounts for it."

"Perhaps," said Jo.

"Spring was cold and muddy and the damned trees took forever to leaf out," her father said in his forthright way. "But summer seems to be making up for it."

The glorious day was suffused with sunshine and the blue heavens seemed limitless. Cowslips and poppies made bright dots in the hayfields, and cows drowsed in the shade of the big trees at the corners of the hedgerows.

Everything seemed to be right where her imagination would have put it. Jo was enchanted.

They arrived in the village shortly after teatime, rattling over the five arches of the Richmond bridge and on to the inn. Joshua, the old family servant, was waiting outside the inn yard to meet them and transfer their luggage into the dogcart. He raised his shaggy eyebrows when the carriage came to a stop beside him.

Jo opened the door and looked out. "Joshua!"

His face broke into a smile framed with deep wrinkles. "Miss! Ye have come home!"

"Yes, at last." She turned back into the carriage to speak to her mother. "Would you mind very much if I went with Joshua? There is so much that I want to see."

"The dogcart is not the most elegant conveyance, Jo."

Her father laughed. "Let the girl do what she wants. How often do they come home once they have left the nest, Mrs. Shy?"

"Hmph, not often enough. But then we were in Bath and the nest was empty. Go, go. Joshua will enjoy the company."

Jo jumped down. The old servant greeted her warmly and took her trunk from the coachman. When he put it in the back of the dogcart, the pony jingled his harness bells and looked her way, hoping for a treat.

"Buttercup!" She stroked his nose and he took a step toward her. "No, I haven't got a treat. It's no use nuzzling my pocket."

"Aye, our Miss Shy is a London lady now, Buttercup. No carrots in her pockets."

"Does he still nip, Joshua?"

"Yes, miss, but he fancies the parson's rump these days. I think Buttercup is a Dissenter."

Josephine laughed. It was wonderful, utterly wonderful, to be home again.

Chapter Thirteen

Her parents settled back into life at The Elms, and the new maid-of-all-work proved satisfactory. Jo returned to Derrydale, walking the last half mile on foot after saying good-bye to Joshua and treating Buttercup, who had brought her there in the dogcart, to a very large carrot.

She entered through the front portal. There was no other word for the great carved doors that swung open with scarcely a creak.

The hall was made of marble and rather chilly. She looked about. There seemed to be no one at home. But considering the vast size of the house, it was possible that they were simply in another wing.

Still, she had expected servants. Jo saw a brass bell upon a table and rang it. It made a dreadful loud noise but no one appeared. She rang it again. At last a very old butler shuffled forth from behind a marble pillar, in no hurry. She saw that he wore carpet slippers that had been embroidered long ago with a now unreadable monogram.

He nodded almost imperceptibly to Jo and crossed the marble floor to her, peering into her face with an expression of comical puzzlement. Then he broke into a wrinkled smile.

"Why, it is Miss Shy. How many years has it been, my dear?"

"Upton?" She recognized him at last. Upton had been old when Daniel was a boy and now he was very, very old. "How nice to see you."

"Lord York said to expect you. I am afraid I fell asleep with the cat in my lap. Dot does not like to be disturbed once she has settled down. But then she is old, like me."

"You don't mean Little Dot? Daniel had a kitten by that name."

"Yes, miss. She is Big Dot now. Likes to eat, she does."

"May I see her?"

Upton's half-closed eyelids rose just a fraction higher. "Yes, if you wish. Lord York gave no particular instructions as to your arrival. Come with me, please."

He shuffled back in the direction he had come from and Jo shortened her free stride so as not to overtake him. They went through a door that led to the house servants' quarters, and Jo saw a rocking chair still rocking slightly, as if its occupant had just gotten up.

"Here is Dot, enjoying the sun."

He shuffled to a basket woven of soft reeds and lined with cloth, which had been placed on the windowsill. It was full of cat: an enormous white cat with a large black dot on her side and black ears.

"She goes from my lap to the basket and back to my lap." Upton stroked the cat's head and she began to purr, turning her head to rub against the old man's hand.

"It is Dot, just as I remember her!" Jo was delighted to see Daniel's pet. "And who is this?" She pointed to an old mastiff of great size sleeping in a corner, his white muzzle propped upon one gigantic paw.

"That is Caesar."

The mastiff opened one eye and looked at her, and shut it again.

"Would you like a cup of tea, Miss Shy? I think the others have gone out to the woods to look for . . ." He paused to think and stroked the cat's head again.

"Yes, Upton? What are they looking for?"

"Mushrooms," he said at last, "I believe it was mushrooms."

"I see . . . Well then, I will have a cup of tea. Thank you."

Upton moved to a table that held an enameled tray decorated with shepherdesses and rotund little sheep. "Mrs. Nottingate has just brought it." He lifted the lid of the white china teapot and let the fragrant steam escape. "It has steeped sufficiently."

"There are two cups. Were you expecting someone?" Jo asked politely.

"No, miss. The cook always puts two cups on the tray. One is for me and one is for Dot. Mrs. Nottingate's little joke." He smiled creakily.

He poured out the tea and indicated a small plate that held buttered scones. "Scone, miss?"

"No, thank you, Upton. Where shall I sit?"

"The armchair is comfy."

She looked before she sat down just to make sure it did not hold a sleeping animal. Upton brought her tea. The cup clattered slightly against the saucer.

"Thank you."

He returned to his rocking chair with a cup in one hand and a scone in the other.

Dot pricked up her ears and shifted inside the basket, putting one paw over the side.

"Stay where you are, you naughty beast," Upton

said to the cat. "I'll not have you upsetting my tea
and nibbling at my breakfast." He smiled at Jo.
"Loves butter, she does."

They sat for a long while in companionable silence, sipping tea. The cat's purr deepened as she
went back to sleep, whiskers twitching, her furry
bulk rising and falling with each breath.

Jo looked at the somnolent Dot with a smile as
she sipped her tea. Then she looked out the window. There were people walking at the edge of the
distant woods. Surely one was Lizzie. The tall redhead stood out a mile away.

"There are the others."

"Hmmm?"

"My friends, and Lord York." She nodded toward the window.

Upton peered at it. "I will take your word for it,
my dear." He had finished his tea and scone, and
he set the cup aside. The sun had reached the rocking chair and he closed his eyes, rocking to and
fro.

The clink of china awakened Dot, who looked
at the old man and seized her chance. She jumped
out of the basket, landing with a thud upon the floor,
and then jumped into his lap. He did not even open
his eyes.

After a minute or two, Jo set down her own cup
very quietly. She might as well go out to meet the
others.

On tiptoe, she left the butler's room and went
back into the marble hall, wondering how she might
get out. There seemed to be no end of doors and
they might lead anywhere.

She chose a likely one and opened it. Drat, a
closet. It held boots. Musty, mildewed boots that had
been carefully put away at least a decade ago. There
were cricket bats and other sporting gear, and an

angler's net on a pole. A large spider had taken up residence in the middle of the net. Jo shivered a little and hastily shut the door.

She opened another.

This was a small room with a window. Well, at least she was a little closer to the outside. She considered climbing out the window and decided against it. Undoubtedly it had not been opened for some time.

The room was a jumble of furniture and miscellaneous items that had once been too good to discard or burn, and were now too brittle or decrepit to use. Someone in a hurry had simply stuffed everything in and left it there, probably years ago.

Jo closed the door. She looked around and counted ten others in various places, but there was no telling which one might lead outside. She decided to stand in the middle of the marble floor, close her eyes, stretch out a hand, spin, and then open whichever door her finger pointed to.

First she looked up. The dome that crowned the marble entry hall was painted with angels riding clouds. They looked down at her with beatific smiles.

She looked around. No one would see her. The house was quite still. She could not hear Upton's rocking chair and was sure he was sound asleep.

Jo closed her eyes and began to spin. She stopped and went to the door she pointed to, opening it wide.

Another closet, quite empty.

Perhaps she ought to go out the front and simply walk around, but the wings of the house went on for some distance and she would never remember her way through the outbuildings and garden of botanical rarities.

She closed her eyes and spun again. When she

stopped, a strong hand clasped hers. Jo opened her eyes wide, feeling very foolish indeed.

"Daniel!"

"Hello, Jo. Whatever are you doing?"

"Trying to find a way out."

"With your eyes closed?" He laughed at her and let go of her hand to chuck her under the chin. "You are a funny one."

She could not blame him for laughing. She looked down and saw that he was carrying his muddy boots. No wonder she had not heard him enter or walk over to her.

"There are so many doors and none of them seems to go anywhere. Spinning around and pointing seemed as good a way as any to pick one."

"I see. Well, allow me to show you the way." He took her arm but stayed where he was, not seeming to be in any hurry.

"Were you with the others?"

He nodded. "Yes, we were gathering mushrooms."

"Upton told me."

"Ah, I am glad he came out to welcome you. He does not always hear the bell. Did you see Dot?"

"Yes, and Caesar. But Dot is no longer little."

Daniel smiled. "Too much butter. Upton spoils her dreadfully. Shall we go?"

"Lead on, my lord."

He guided her to a corridor that she had not noticed. It was narrow and they could not quite walk side by side without his thigh brushing hers. She rather liked the feeling and did not pull away.

"I don't remember this."

"Of course not. Upton never let my friends play in the hall and you were not here very often. Terence and I went in and out by the kitchen door around the back."

"Ah."

They came to the door at the end of the corridor and Lord York opened it with his free hand.

"There they are."

The little party of mushroom gatherers was coming over a rise. They were closer than they had been when Jo had seen them through the kitchen window but not that close.

"Lizzie was afraid they would be lost without me, but I went ahead. Ginny is fearless and even Lizzie can spot a house the size of this one. And your cousin is not a missish sort."

"Not at all. Penelope is intrepid and intelligent, though she is somewhat shortsighted." Jo was eager to see her and wondered how Penelope was getting on. It had taken a week to get her parents established and comfortable in the cottage, which had needed a great deal of airing out and dusting by the maid and Jo. There had been no note sent from Derrydale during that time.

It had seemed best to separate Penelope from the Shys upon the party's arrival. Feelings had been running high on both sides, and Jo had been afraid that Penelope might blurt out the truth in an anguished moment. If Mrs. Shy could disapprove so thoroughly of a few kisses, Jo could not imagine what the old lady would say or do if she knew that the unmarried Penelope was with child.

Come to think of it, Jo wondered what Lord York would say or do. He was considerably less priggish than he had seemed to her at first, but she would not dare to confide in him on that subject.

She looked up. He was watching Ginny get over a stile, nimble as always. Penelope and Lizzie stayed on the other side of it, seeming flummoxed.

Penelope seemed to be listening to Ginny's instructions and climbed awkwardly over the stile, catching her dress upon it and tugging it free.

Lizzie stood where she was, bellowing like an ill-tempered cow.

"I suppose she will not climb," Lord York said. "And she is very careful of that damned dress. Not the sort of thing one wears to gather mushrooms, but I think she imagined herself doing it onstage, singing all the while."

Jo laughed under her breath, just in case the breeze should carry the sound to Lizzie. She watched Penelope and Ginny reach out their hands to Lizzie, encouraging her.

At last Lizzie put a foot upon the first rung of the stile and went over it, basket upon her arm.

The singer's dress was unharmed, but the handle of her basket caught and mushrooms tumbled out of it. Jo saw rather than heard Lizzie's gasp, and then laughed again as the singer began to stamp upon the fallen mushrooms in a fit of pique.

Lord York grinned. "She is like a child sometimes."

"Yes."

He looked down at Jo. "Were you going to tell me again that she has a good heart? I know that. But oh, what a terrible temper."

"Indeed it is. I am glad that it has never been directed at me."

"No, but those mushrooms are getting the worst of it."

"Lizzie, stop!" they heard Ginny call faintly. "Ye'll ruin yer fine shoes! Come along."

The three women quickened their pace and came closer. Ginny and Penelope saw Lord York and Jo, and waved to them, but Lizzie was watching where she walked, grumbling loudly and pausing to catch her breath in between grumbles.

"Blast my bloody . . . fine shoes! I . . . have had . . . quite enough . . . of this rural frolic . . . and I hate . . . gathering my own . . . food! I want . . . to go back to London . . . where . . . oh, dear, I have stepped in something awful . . . where they bring it to you . . . on a tray!" Lizzie looked up at last and spied Lord York and Jo. "Oh, hello. Sorry about the mushrooms, but they filled their baskets to the brim."

"How nice to see you, Lizzie," Jo said impishly.

"The same to you, my pet. How are your parents? Snug in their sweet little cottage?" Lizzie swept past, not waiting for an answer. "Good, good."

Jo stepped forth to greet her cousin, very pleased to see that Penelope had roses in her cheeks and seemed a great deal happier than when Jo had seen her last. They embraced. Jo and Ginny clasped hands, and shared a silent laugh at Lizzie's expense.

"Herself is in a swivet," Ginny said, "but that can't be helped."

"I think we will have to send her back to the theater," Lord York said. "Sunshine and fresh air are very bad for her."

"Oh, no, Lord York," Ginny said. "If she goes, then I must go with her. Keep her here another day."

"Very well, but I have sent for Tom and the wagon."

"Why, sir? There will be room enough in the carriage."

"Oh, you will all ride in the carriage. But Terence has asked that we send some of our old furniture, and other odds and ends. He thinks he might be able to use it. There is enough rubbish like that in the house, God knows."

"Very well." Ginny looked disappointed.

"But you are welcome to return whenever you wish, Mrs. Goodchurch."

"Thank you, sir!" She dropped a curtsy and followed Lizzie's path to the house quite quickly, as if she feared he might change his mind.

Jo took Penelope's arm. "My dear cousin Upton gave me a cup of tea but perhaps you would like some refreshment. And we have not talked for a week. You do not mind if we wander off, do you, Daniel? There seems to be no end of drawing rooms in your house."

He bowed ever so slightly. "Not at all. Just tell the tweeny where you will be so Mrs. Nottingate can send her up with a tray. Most of the servants are too old to walk much."

"I understand." His regard for them touched her.

"Penelope's bedchamber connects to a very pleasant little room where you two can be quite private and giggle to your hearts' content."

"Thank you, Lord York," Penelope said.

Jo heard the sadness underneath her cousin's polite tone. Indeed, there was nothing to giggle about. But Jo was very glad to be at Derrydale with her.

The tweeny, a strapping maidservant of fifteen or so, set down the tray between them. Mrs. Nottingate had provided heartier fare—indeed, it would serve them well for lunch.

Penelope looked at it a little queasily when the tweeny had left.

"You must eat a little, Penny."

"I have been sick every morning. Ginny is in the next room and she hears, I think. But she does not ask questions."

"She would not."

They sat for a minute or two in silence. Penelope would not meet Jo's eye.

"How have you been? Have you decided upon anything—where you will go or who will go with you?"

Penelope shook her head. "I can only say that I will remain in England. I am not inclined to take an extended tour of the Continent, as ladies in my circumstances do."

"Then you are not going to Egypt."

Penelope smiled. "No, that was a wild fantasy. I scarcely knew what I was saying that night. I could not think straight. The journey from Bath was so wearying and your dear mama had not one kind word to say, though I was grateful that she did not scold me. And again, Jo, I was—am—so very sorry for the trouble I caused her. And you . . ." She trailed off.

Jo laid a hand upon her cousin's arm. "Mama is quite recovered from the shock of finding out that you allowed yourself to be kissed, I assure you. As for the rest, she will never know unless you decide to tell her."

Penelope nodded and folded her hands in her lap. A solitary tear rolled down her cheek.

"Penny, listen to me. Whatever happens, I will be by your side. You are not alone in this."

"Jo, do not speak so. You are young and unmarried. My foolish mistake is my own. I cannot allow you to be tainted by scandal."

"I care nothing for what people say. You are my friend."

"Thank you," Penny said in a whisper. "May I stay with you in London for now? I cannot go home. There is no one there but the servants, but they will talk. Everyone will know."

"Of course you may stay with me, for as long as you like."

"We will have to tell Terence," Penelope pointed out.

"He is impossible to shock. My dear brother is rather, ah, unconventional. Yes, that is the very word he used to describe himself." Jo rattled on, not wanting to reveal that she had already told Terence. "And as for scandal, I hear a thousand scandalous things a day at the theater."

"I am sure that Miss Loudermilk says half of them." The ghost of a smile touched Penny's quivering lips.

"Yes, but I find that I am no longer shocked. My dear mama would not like to hear me say it, but words are only words. I find a refreshing lack of hypocrisy among the theater folk. They are vain, quarrelsome, and free with their affections, as my brother puts it, but they are not hypocrites."

"Well then, I ought to go upon the stage," Penelope said wryly.

"Oh, dear me, no. Promise me you will not."

"I was only joking. I have no talent, and no inclination to do so, Jo. But Miss Loudermilk says that you do. You are not considering joining the company of players, are you?"

"Certainly not."

"She says you are always at the theater."

Jo nodded. "That is true. I was very cross when my mother said she was descending upon us, for I have never told her of that, and Terence would not. No, I help him when I can, and I also assist Lizzie with her vocal practice."

"She seems . . ." Penny took a moment to find the right word. "Indestructible."

"That's our Lizzie. Now eat something, Penny. You must keep your strength up."

She watched Penelope stick a fork in a piece of

country ham and nibble on it as if it were a child's sweet on a stick.

"It is very good ham," she said after a minute. "Have some yourself, Jo."

"I will. I must set a good example."

"Too late for that," Penelope said.

Jo laughed. "You are quite right. Now take little bites so you won't get sick."

"Yes, mother." Penelope took her time about finishing the ham. She ate half of a buttered roll and nibbled on a sprig of watercress.

"This was growing by the river. We had a pleasant picnic there. And that reminds me—Lord York said that you and he are hoping to find a frog that lives there. Old Gus, I believe he called it, and he said, I quote, that it is an amphibian of legendary size and cunning. He wants to catch it. But what will he do with it if he does?"

"Let it go, I expect. He is very kind."

Penelope nibbled on another sprig of watercress. "Do you love him, Jo?"

She looked up, startled. "What?"

"You talk about him with such tenderness. And he too is always at the theater, according to Lizzie. Is that another reason you spend so much time there?"

"Perhaps," Jo said, blushing.

Jo went down to the river that very afternoon. She found the right place easily enough. Daniel had posted a flag, as he'd said he would.

He had gone to the trouble of sending a written invitation to her room, delivered by the young lad who had scampered about after Upton, when the old butler was not sleeping, and ran errands for him.

She pulled the invitation from her basket and read it again.

The presence of Miss Josephine Shy

is respectfully requested

by 2:00 o'clock at the river

(a red flag wil be posted at the spot)

for a matinee performance of

"Good Old Gus"

Refreshments will be provided.

She settled herself upon the riverbank and slipped off her shoes. She had come a bit early and felt inclined to go barefoot. The grass was delightfully warm.

Jo drew up her legs under her dress and rested her chin on her knees, staring into the water. It eddied around mossy rocks and flowed on, sparkling in the summer sun. She could not quite see beneath its surface . . . but could that unmoving lump be Gus? No, it was a submerged rock.

She looked where the water was still. Of course, she thought, if she did glimpse the monstrous frog, she would not do anything that might startle him. Daniel would not forgive her if the Great Uncatchable Sir Slippery escaped him once more.

If the legendary frog still lived.

She saw bubbles rise upon the water and pop one by one. Was that Gus? No, it was a pike, gliding through the water, narrow and sleek.

She jumped a little when a picnic basket landed on the blanket beside her.

"Hello, Jo. Have you seen him yet?"

"No. Are you sure that old Gus is still here? What is the life span of a frog?"

"I have no idea. But this is the right spot."

He sat down beside her and crossed his legs, thought better of it, and removed his boots. They were old and worn, and came off easily. He left on his stockings, which were nice and white and new, she noticed.

"Shall we eat first? Are you hungry?"

"Not yet."

"May I tempt you?"

"Please do."

He unfastened the leather-and-peg clasp of the basket and looked inside. "Mrs. Nottingate always does a good picnic. There are rolls, and cake, and a jar of berries." He took these out. "What is in the damp napkin? Oh, cheese. Of course. Two bottles of beer. And there is a ham someone has been hacking at. It looks familiar. I believe I made its acquaintance at breakfast."

Jo giggled. "So did I. It is very good. I would not mind a bit more in a little while."

"We must save the bone for Caesar. He expects it. No doubt he has been dreaming of it. We must render unto Caesar the things that are Caesar's, and all that."

"Yes. He is a fine old dog."

"He came to Derrydale some years ago. I am afraid everyone at Derrydale is on the old side."

"You are not, Daniel."

"No, but taking care of it all makes me feel old sometimes. I have had to close off many rooms to save money on firewood and coal, and the plaster is falling in many more. I cannot afford to fix everything at once. It is a struggle to keep up appearances and my brother is no help."

"I see."

He let out a sigh. "Gerald and I do not like each other. He often let me know when we were boys that he would be quite happy if the gypsies took me or a fever finished me off."

"But surely—"

"In time, I came to feel that way about him. But he is healthy enough, though the only exercise he ever gets is throwing dice and fanning out his cards. He would stake Derrydale at the gaming table if he felt like it."

"Oh."

"The estate is his—our—only source of income. And it is mortgaged to the hilt."

She gave him a long look. "But you would not sell the place, would you?"

"It is not mine to sell, Jo."

"No, of course not," she murmured.

"Gerald expects me to manage it for him. Derrydale is dear to me and so I do. But to answer your question . . . no. I would never sell it."

He leaned back on his elbows and stretched out his legs.

"Let us talk of other things. Are you happy here, Josephine?"

"Yes, of course. I quite enjoy being home."

"Do you miss London?"

"Not yet."

He rolled over to look at her.

"Do you miss the theater?"

"Not at all. It has done us all good to get away from that dusty cave and its endless corridors."

"Lizzie doesn't think so."

Josephine flopped onto her front and ran her fingers through the warm grass. "She was born in a stage trunk or so she says."

"Really?" Lord York said. "Then her mother must have been a very small woman."

"You are being silly."

"That is because I suddenly feel silly. Wonderfully silly. I have not a care in the world at the moment."

"What about Gerald?"

"To hell with Gerald. I am sorry that I mentioned him. Forgive me."

"You are allowed to complain," Jo said. "He sounds horrible. More like your enemy than a brother."

"I insist that we change the subject!"

"Very well. What about Gus? Your manly honor requires you to catch him."

"Oh, yes, good old Gus." He rolled back and sat up, taking off his stockings and unfastening his breeches at the knees to roll them up. "Here I go."

He strode down to the river, a fine figure of a man in breeches and shirt. Jo looked with open admiration at his back and his bottom and his strong legs. There was no one there to chide her for doing so.

He stuck a toe into the water. "Ah, most refreshing." He waded in. "Slippery, though." He stood for a bit, getting his balance as he turned to face her with a grin. Then he looked down into the water. "I see everything but a frog. Minnows. And little creeping things. And—that was a pike!"

"I saw that pike."

"He is too young to be worth catching, and I have no tackle."

"I saw an angler's net in one of the closets."

"Really? I was wondering where that was. Did it have a hole in it?"

"I don't remember. The net is presently occupied by a very large spider."

"Oh," he said absentmindedly, looking down into the water again.

Jo studied him from the front. Even better. What a handsome man he was. And that smile. Oh, dear, perhaps she should not have come out alone with him. It was dreadfully improper—and she realized that she did not care in the least.

"Come to me, Jo."

"I beg your pardon?"

"Do not talk in that missish way and do not beg my pardon. You want to wade in the water."

"I do not."

"You do."

Their eyes met for a long moment, and Jo could not look away.

"Sweet Jo," he said softly, "there is no one to see. If you get a bit wet, the sun will soon dry you."

"Turn your back."

"Why?'

"I must roll up my drawers."

He shook his head sadly. "Must I look away?"

"Yes."

He turned his back to her and she stayed sitting to roll up her linen drawers to the knee, standing up to roll them a little higher. Then she bent down to take the hem of her dress in hand, and straightened.

He had been watching her all the while over his shoulder.

"You are not a gentleman!"

"No." He grinned rather wolfishly. "Not always."

"Do you promise not to splash me?"

"I will not, I promise. But the rocks are slippery, Jo. You must be careful."

She walked down to the riverbank and stuck in a toe just as he had done. "Oo, that is indeed refreshing." She stepped into the water. "But I can see much better when I look straight down. The water is as clear as crystal. Look—over there! Is that a frog?"

He looked where she pointed. "Yes, but it is a very small one."

"Perhaps it is a son or daughter of Old Gus."

Daniel reached down to grab it but the frog jumped and landed a few feet away with a tiny plop. It disappeared under the water.

"You may be right. It is just as wily."

He put his hands on his knees to see where it had gone.

"Ah, now watch. There is a trick to hunting frogs. One must be swift . . . and stealthy."

He made another grab but came up empty-handed.

"Damnation, he got away."

Jo looked down into the water. Something had brushed against her foot. But she saw nothing. She kept looking down and was rewarded by the sight of a small frog circling her ankle. Very slowly she reached down, grabbed just ahead of where it was swimming, and came up with it, holding it with utmost gentleness in her closed fist.

The little frog gulped and blinked. It scrabbled a bit at her fingers, then stopped. She felt its cool belly touch her palm as it breathed and gulped.

"Very good, Jo!" Daniel waded over and stroked the frog between the eyes. It gulped and closed them.

"Do frogs enjoy that?" she asked.

"I don't know, but it does make them close their eyes."

"I expect it wants to be back in the cool water. Good-bye, little friend." She bent down and opened her hand. It hung in the water for a fraction of a second, then swam away, kicking its back legs with all its might.

"I confess I feel ashamed. You have caught a frog and I have caught nothing but a leaf between my toes." He leaned down to pull it out and let it float away upon the shallow water. Then he dried his hand upon his breeches and reached out to her, saying nothing more.

Jo took his hand. "Do you remember that my nursemaid never would let me go in the water? I feel quite bold."

"Does you good. You look very pretty, you know."

They waded on until the water became deeper and colder.

"Shall we turn back? I do not think we will find Old Gus here. He probably prefers to be where it is warm, like all old creatures do."

"Yes."

They turned around together, taking measured and deliberate steps to avoid slipping or pulling each other over.

"This is like a dance," he said.

"It is a funny one." Jo giggled. They returned the way they had come, keeping an eye out for other frogs, but they saw none.

"Hunting frogs is hard work and I find that I am ravenous. Let us go back."

"We have been in the water for only a few minutes, and we have not caught Gus."

"You mean that I have not caught Gus. He is too big a frog for you to capture. No, I reserve that honor for myself."

"I see. Well then, you must build up your strength."

They waded to the bank and scrambled up it. Jo

dropped the hem of her dress the second she was out of the water.

Settling themselves upon the blanket once more, they did justice to Mrs. Nottingate's picnic lunch, and then lay back to digest and watch the clouds drift by.

"Shall we go back in?" she asked.

"No. Never mind Old Gus. Or my manly honor. I am too happy to hunt at the moment. You make me happy, Jo."

"Oh . . ." If only life could always be like this, she thought. Free. And easy. And not at all respectable or proper.

Jo was determined to enjoy every moment of their brief idyll in the sun. She would have far too much to fret over when they arrived in London on the morrow. For now—just for now—she put her worries aside.

She was drowsy and closed her eyes for a few moments. When she opened them, she saw Daniel raise one hand and count on his fingers.

"What are you doing?"

"Counting the kisses I have given you."

"You will need two hands."

He rolled over and stroked her hair. "You looked so lovely lying there. I did not want to disturb your sweet slumber."

"Oh, please don't talk like that," she said, shielding her eyes from the sun and laughing.

"Like what?"

"Like one of Hugh's silly characters. Sweet slumber, indeed. I was only napping."

"Are you completely awake?"

"Yes, why?"

"Never let it be said that I took advantage of a sleeping woman." He pulled her into his arms and kissed her quite passionately. Several times.

"You are supposed to push me away, Jo."

"I don't want to."

"I will have to marry you, you know."

"Is that a proposal?"

He held her close and nuzzled her neck. "It is. If you don't mind marrying a second son with no money and no prospects."

"Not at all. I love you."

He rose up on his elbows.

"Are you quite sure?"

"Yes, Daniel."

"Then there is nothing more to say, except that I love you."

"Oh . . ."

He kissed her again.

Chapter Fourteen

The promised musicale would begin in an hour. Lizzie sat at a gilt harpsichord, banging its ivory keys with vigor and warming up with a naughty song. Ginny told her in a fierce whisper to stop when Upton came through the doors of the music room, leading the way for the tweeny.

The girl carried a tray filled with glasses and a pitcher of lemonade that looked most refreshing. The day had been warm and the French doors of the music room were flung open to catch the evening breeze.

"Our last night here," Ginny said. "Seems a shame to leave. London will be much hotter."

"I can't wait," Lizzie said, experimenting with a few crescendos and diminuendos.

"Be careful with that there instrument, Lizzie. I am sure it is old and valuable."

"It is out of tune."

"That doesn't mean ye can bang upon it in that disrespectful way. Ah, here is Lord York."

He entered through the far doors on the other side of the room with Josephine on his arm.

"Don't they make a handsome couple," Ginny said admiringly.

Lizzie closed the harpsichord's lid. "Yes, they do. I sometimes wonder if they are in love. If I were Jo, I would not let that one get away."

"Whatever do ye mean?"

"It is plain to see that he adores her."

Ginny watched Lord York and Josephine stroll out the French doors together. "Yes, ye're right. But she might not be so sure of her feelings for him. She is young yet."

"Pshaw," Lizzie said, "she should not shilly-shally. We must encourage them. Someone else might snap him up from under her nose."

"If he truly loves her, that will not happen."

Lizzie snorted. "It happens all the time."

"Now, Lizzie, not another peep. They are coming back."

Lord York and Jo came through the French doors. She was holding a pink blossom of some sort and her eyes were glowing.

"Aha. She looks radiant. He has given her a flower."

"A ring would be better. Swear eternal love, post the banns, and get it over with."

"Oh, Lizzie," the wardrobe mistress chided her, "there is more to it than that. He is a deliberate sort o' man. Step by step, that is how he likes to do things."

"You seem to have become great friends with him."

Ginny, remembering the part she had played in their last visit to a garden, hid a smile. "P'raps."

Lord York and Jo walked toward them, and Lizzie opened the harpsichord lid again. She played a sprightly air.

"Why, you play beautifully, Miss Loudermilk. That

is a country dance, one of my late mother's favorites," Lord York said. "I am afraid the instrument is sadly out of tune, however."

"I noticed." She launched into some interesting variations, absorbed in the music.

Ginny looked at the young couple, beaming. She caught Lord York's eye and moved her feet as if she were dancing. He took the hint.

"Ah, may I have this dance, Miss Shy?"

"It would be my pleasure, sir."

"The pleasure is all mine."

He straightened, bowed, and took her hand, and they moved into interesting variations of their own, through a waltz and a minuet and others, until Jo was breathless and rosy.

"Do you know," Ginny whispered to Lizzie, "I don't think they need any encouragement."

Lizzie looked up and studied the dancing couple. They moved in step, following each other's rhythm to perfection as they gazed into each other's eyes with obvious love.

"Hmmm, perhaps you are right. Well, let's see if their newly budded love survives our opening night. Nothing like a theatrical production to bring out the worst in people."

"Hush, Lizzie. I don't think so. That looks like true love to me, and the best is yet to come."

"If you say so."

Lord York and Josephine ended their dance and bowed to each other, grinning like fools.

Ginny handed round the lemonade, and they made merry until the moon came up.

Tom Higgins pulled up at the Derrydale stables and let the groom see to the horses and the wagon. They would not be leaving until tomorrow, of course, but Terence had instructed him to get an early start, and roll Miss Loudermilk out of bed himself if he had to.

Tom had no intention of doing any such thing. Lizzie would probably bite him on the ankle. No, they would leave when she was ready and not afore, he thought.

The groom directed him to the front of the house, but Tom chose to ramble a little under the full moon and stretch his legs. He could hear music coming from somewhere, and Lizzie's glorious, full voice in song. A lighter, sweeter soprano joined hers. Miss Jo, no doubt.

Tom bumped into an animal he had not seen at first. It didn't bark. Well, no it wouldn't. It seemed to be a sheep. A few other sheep drifted closer, looking at him with mild eyes.

Interesting. He had seen a great many sheep upon the journey to Richmond and he supposed these belonged to Lord York. Gentlemen kept them to graze upon their lawns, he knew.

He stood still, not wanting to startle the silly beasts. They drifted away, white and dreamlike in the moonlight. It occurred to him that they would look very nice upon the Covent Garden stage, in just such a bluish light, in the climactic scene of *The Shepherdess*.

"Add a touch of that there verisimilitude, they would," he said softly.

He sat down, and pulled up a few stalks of tender grass. "Here, sheepy sheepy. Come, then. Come to me." The stupidest-looking of the lot responded to his coaxing and turned around.

He supposed it was female. It had no horns. The creature stood there and eyed him warily.

"Here, sheepy sheepy."

Wonder of wonders, the ewe came to take the grass from his hand. She chewed and swallowed, and cast a loving look upon him. Or was it a hungry look?

Tom didn't care. If this one was willing to eat from his hand, the others might also. And if he could hide them in the wagon and bring them to London, he would set them loose upon the stage and give Lizzie Loudermilk her much-deserved comeuppance.

A gleeful grin spread across his face.

The morning of the next day dawned bright and clear. The women bustled around the carriage, checking to make sure that every valise, case, portmanteau, sacque, and reticule had been brought down from their rooms.

"I will never understand why women travel with so many things," Lord York said. "I myself require only one bag."

"Pooh pooh," said Lizzie, "you have an entire house in Mayfair to hold your kit. It is easy for you to travel light, my lord. Hold your tongue."

"Lizzie!" Ginny said.

Lord York only laughed. "I find I have grown accustomed to her abuse, Mrs. Goodchurch. You need not scold her. Besides, our opening night is not far away. She must be nervous."

Lizzie raised an eyebrow. "Me? Nervous? No. Never. I just want to get back to London. But I do love the country. The mushrooms were unforgettable. And the musical entertainment was second to none, even if I did have to provide it myself. Do have that harpsichord tuned, my lord."

"Oh, get in the carriage, ye bad-mannered hussy!" Ginny cried. She practically shoved Lizzie through the door, then clambered in after her. "Come, Penelope!"

Jo's cousin walked slowly to the carriage, again looking somewhat unwell. "Thank you, Lord York. I did enjoy my stay, even if I did not leave my room very often. I was—"

"No need to explain," he said gallantly. "I do hope you will return, and soon."

Penelope looked at Jo. "Yes, mayhap."

Jo helped her in and picked up her bag. "Ready, my lord?"

"My what?" he said very softly.

"My love," she whispered.

"That's better. Let us go." He gave her a hand up and entered last of all.

The return journey was wearisome. The road to London was crowded with wagons heaped with vegetables and fruits, and travelers from the South. The four women went to sleep one by one, Jo last of all. But not Lord York.

He studied her sweet, dreaming face and imagined what it would be like to see her head upon a pillow next to his, sharing the sensual intimacies of a happy marriage.

He had no doubt their marriage would prove happy. Jo was a level-headed, loving girl, for all her unconventionality. Her parents were a highly proper old pair, who might be surprised to hear of their sudden engagement, but Daniel could smooth over any ruffled feelings when the time came to tell them.

But how to tell Terence? *He* might only shrug and wish them both well. Terence was decidedly casual about too many things. Of course, Jo could not help her brother's devil-may-care attitude. Yet they were alike in their unfailing kindness to others.

Jo was not always completely respectful to Daniel,

of course, but that was to be expected. She was in love. With him. She had said so. Reciprocated love was so much nicer than the other sort. He considered himself a very lucky man.

Most importantly, she had said yes, even though his proposal had been unplanned. He had gone down to the river with little else in mind besides enjoying an impromptu picnic with her.

Of course he had taken great trouble with the invitation, ripping up five drafts for minor errors in penmanship before producing the final version, which Upton's lad had delivered.

He had instructed the boy as to which door to knock upon, not wanting the invitation to fall into the wrong hands. Not that Ginny or Lizzie, cheerfully cavalier about morality like all theater folk, would have scolded Jo or told her not to go alone. No, it was Jo's cousin Penelope he was not sure of.

The girl seemed somewhat odd and distant, staying in her room for the first several days and not coming down to dinner, offering only vague excuses. But she had brightened up considerably when Jo had returned to Derrydale.

Daniel supposed that she would be staying with Jo and her brother in the Guilford Street house. At least Penelope was a more seemly companion for Jo than Lizzie Loudermilk. Her dowdy dresses and disheveled air, plus the spectacles she occasionally wore, made her a perfect chaperone. He was glad to know that most of Jo's near relations were thoroughly respectable. Certainly no one would ever expect Penelope of romantic inclinations, though the girl might be pretty enough with a little help.

He smiled to himself. He supposed Lizzie could do the honors, if it came to that. The singer was a formidably attractive female when she wanted to be—and sometimes just formidable.

But her best friend, Ginny Goodchurch, was a treasure. He wondered if she might be persuaded to leave the theater and come to Derrydale once he and Jo commenced setting up their nursery.

He looked forward to begetting a tribe of little Daniels and Josephines—as many as his future wife might want. They had not discussed the subject of children but he assumed that she would want them.

The thought of her angelic voice singing a lullaby over a cradle made his heart contract. How dear she had become to him in only a matter of weeks!

Daniel looked out the window to see the moon high above the trees. The blue light it cast let him see the occupants of the carriage well enough but it was Jo's face his eyes lingered on.

Sweet dreams, my darling. Had he been able to, he would have kissed her soft cheek. At last he drifted off . . .

The carriage hit a bump in the road and he awoke with a start. Penelope did too. She looked distinctly unwell, even by moonlight.

He could see beads of perspiration upon her forehead. She clamped a hand over her mouth.

Daniel leaned forward. "Shall I wake Jo?" he asked softly.

But Penelope was already shaking her cousin by the shoulder and whispering something in her ear.

Jo's eyes flew open. "Yes, Penny. Daniel, ask the coachman to stop."

He nodded and rapped the stick placed in the carriage for that purpose upon the carriage roof. The coachman slowed the horses and pulled gradually to the side of the road, roundly cursing a wagon that had not moved out of their way quickly enough.

"She is going to be sick," Jo said in a measured tone.

He admired Jo's aplomb in such trying circumstances but even so. "Jo, it is dark outside. Allow me to help her—"

"No!" Penelope took her hand off her mouth long enough to say that and just as quickly covered it again. The two women scrambled out. Lizzie and Ginny looked about groggily, awakened by the motion.

"Why have we stopped?" Ginny yawned.

"Jo asked me to." Lord York did not look outside the window or the door, which was swinging open. He could hear Penelope being very sick indeed.

"What is the matter with her?" Lizzie said.

"Which her?" Lord York asked politely.

"Whichever one is puking."

"That would be Penelope, I believe."

"Poor girl," Ginny said sympathetically.

She reached out to help Jo and Penny back in. Lord York took a good look at Penelope. Her full bosom . . . he realized with a start that it had grown fuller in the ten days she had been with them. Her luminous, troubled eyes. Her queasy expression. He looked at Jo, who did not look away. In fact, she glared at him.

"If you say one word, Daniel—"

"Jo, dear, whatever is the matter with Penny?" Ginny asked.

Penelope made an *urp*ing noise and scrambled outside again.

"It's clear enough," Lizzie said dryly. "The girl is pregnant."

Chapter Fifteen

"Consider the situation a test of your character," Jo said firmly.

Daniel, who had been looking out the window of her drawing room, turned around to face her.

"*My* character?" he asked. "It seems to me that the situation, as you call it, is a test of Penelope's character. Which she has failed."

Jo sighed. "I really want to kick you, Daniel. Give me one good reason not to kick you. In five seconds. One. Two. Three. Four."

"Five. Kick me if you like. I refuse to give in."

She threw up her hands in utter frustration. "Don't you see? I could be in Penelope's predicament if I had not stopped you when we were kissing."

"Which episode of kissing are you referring to?"

"A few days ago, in Derrydale. I have not kissed you since. You do not deserve to be kissed."

"What have I done, Jo? I ask you, what have I done?"

"You have decided that my cousin is somehow to blame for what has happened to her."

Daniel looked at her levelly. "Penelope was not ravished by Zeus or some such being."

"No-o," Jo said slowly, "but she is, or was, so innocent, Daniel. And so lonely for so long. We cannot change what has happened. I am sure she wishes she had never seen Oliver's face."

"Is that his name?"

"Yes."

"Does he have a last name?"

"I don't know."

"Does Penelope know?"

"I really will kick you."

He backed away slightly.

"I am sure that she does know his last name, but he has disappeared. Now that she is with child—and frightened to death, I might add—I feel it is my duty to help her in every way."

"It is simply not respectable!" he cried.

"Fie upon respectability! You were rolling me around in the grass by the river! You invited me to a clandestine meeting and called it a matinee! In honor of a frog! What was respectable about that?"

"Nothing," he admitted. "But I am going to marry you."

"Maybe, maybe not."

He crossed the room and took her by the shoulders. "What are you saying, Jo?"

"I insist that you show Penelope the same consideration and courtesy that you extended to her before you knew of this. She is still my cousin. She is still a good woman."

"She is still pregnant. Am I supposed to stroll upon the streets of London with my beloved fiancée and her enceinte, unmarried cousin? I tell you, I cannot do it."

Jo stamped her foot. "Penelope has no desire to go out in public even now. She is simply too miserable. And I expect she will feel even more ashamed when she begins to show. But I have offered to let her stay under this roof for as long as she needs to."

Lord York raised an eyebrow. "Does Terence know of this?"

"Yes."

"And what did he say?"

"He wants to help her."

"Dear God. How?"

"Do you know, I suggested that he marry her. I was distraught when she first confided in me and not thinking straight—"

"It is not such a bad idea as all that."

Jo kicked him.

"Ow!"

"You deserved that."

He took a deep breath. "Perhaps I did. I am sorry, Jo. I do love you. And I hope that you still love me. You do, don't you?"

"You are a prig."

"I am a realist. Penelope will receive the cut direct wherever she goes, despite her wealth. Polite society will have nothing to do with her. And that, my dear Jo, will mean that they will have nothing to do with *you*. You are an unmarried girl and very close in age to Penelope. People will assume the worst."

She shrugged. "Perhaps not. I am the daughter of a country vicar. No one knows who I am."

"But they know me."

Jo looked him up and down. "You are a second son. You have no more standing than I do."

Lord York sighed. "I see no way out of this. I must confess, I thought that working in the theater would prove dangerous to your reputation. I never expected that this—oh, I cannot think! But you must understand that Penelope's rash act reflects upon all the family. Especially you."

Jo folded her arms across her bosom and tapped her foot upon the carpet. "Then marry me. Now."

"What?"

"If we are married, then no one can say I am not respectable."

"I do not have a special license and it will take a little time to procure one. Not to mention the extra expense."

"Pay a call upon the archbishop. You said he was a friend of your father's."

"Well, yes, he is . . . but I simply cannot storm into the rectory and . . . no reasonable person goes about demanding such things of archbishops, to say nothing of the explanation I will have to make. I cannot do it."

"Do you love me?"

"Yes!" Daniel howled.

"Do you want to lose me?"

"No!"

Jo tapped her foot harder. "Go!"

They were married the very next morning. Penelope sat in the first pew, with Ginny holding her hand. Lizzie attended as well, wearing a hat so big no one could see her face. Everybody cried, even Terence. But not Lord York.

"Wake up, my dear wife. It is very late. The moon has set and sunrise is only an hour away."

Jo stirred but did not open her eyes.

"That narrow sofa does not look comfortable. You are sleeping in your clothes. And your shoes."

"I know," she yawned.

"Would you like to come to bed?"

"Is it perfectly respectable?" she murmured. "Will the members of polite society approve?"

"I have not asked them."

"Where is Penny?"

"She has gone to stay in Lizzie's town house."

Jo sat up. "That is not at all respectable."

"All she said was, 'In for a penny, in for a pound.' I think she meant it as a joke. She is coming back. But this is our wedding night. I thought we might try to enjoy it. I have done as you requested. We are man and wife. I love you and I want you in my bed. Now."

"Isn't it my bed? Which house am I in?"

Lord York picked Jo up in his arms. "The one on Guilford Street. You won, remember? Wake up, Jo."

"I am awake. Partially. Go that way." She pointed. "Are you strong enough to carry me up all those stairs?"

"Yes."

She curled her arms around his neck. "What shall we do? Did you have anything particular in mind?"

"Nothing respectable."

Jo giggled

The rehearsals resumed.

Terence and Lord York sat together in the box nearest the stage, watching Molly fly over the castaway, shrieking with glee.

"My sister is a strong-willed girl, Daniel. But I think you will be very happy together. Jo is the warmest-hearted, most loyal person I know."

"One problem remains."

"Penelope?"

"Yes."

"I am working on a solution." Terence leaned back in his chair. "Molly, do not swing so close to Andy's head! You might decapitate him and then we would have to get another castaway!"

"Ow, Mr. Shy! It is Arlecchi-chi-chi-nooooooooo who controls the wire! Tell *him* that!"

She sailed out over the pit, waving to Terence and Daniel as she went by the box. Terence yawned.

"Oh, by the way, we have added another sketch. Would you like to see McNeel's drawings for the set?"

Daniel looked at his brother-in-law with astonishment. "Is that necessary? The show is already almost five hours long."

"But the crowd will love this one." Terence sat upright again. "Come along. We shall pay a call on McNeel." Molly swooped by once more. "She seems to have the hang of it. So to speak."

Chapter Sixteen

Daniel and Terence studied the drawings that McNeel was spreading out upon a table in his workshop. He unrolled them one by one, placing and replacing smooth stones at the corners to keep the drawings from rolling back up.

McNeel had saved the best for last, and unrolled it with a flourish.

"Now that is exactly what I had in mind!" Terence said. "What do you think, Daniel? Is that not a Chamber of Wonders?"

"I suppose so," Daniel said. "But where will we get the money to build this? That is an elaborate set."

"Ah, here is Hugh!" Terence said, not answering Daniel's question. "Let us hear what he thinks."

Hugh came over and looked down at the drawing, noting the Egyptian pillars with palm-frond capitals and the row of sarcophagi that stood beneath them.

"Very good," Hugh said excitedly. "The mummies can pop out of the giant coffin things, dance a bit—we will have to be careful about the bandages not dragging—and sing in harmony. Oh, I can see it. Very colorful. But why are we adding a new scene?"

Terence shrugged. "Why not? *The Castaway* is a bit depressing. Egypt is in the headlines now. A fearless explorer just dug up another pharaoh and a lot of his jewelry."

"Ought to let the auld bugger rest in peace, if ye ask me," McNecl said.

"There's a song in that," murmured Hugh. He sang under his breath. "*Let the auld bugger . . . let the auld bugger . . .* Damnation, nothing rhymes with bugger."

"Hugger," McNeel said.

"Won't work. Mummy might be easier."

"Rummy," McNeel said. "Tummy. Chummy. Dummy. Gummy."

"Please stop," said Terence distractedly.

"Sorry."

"Quite all right. Hugh, remember, we want a cheerful tune. Send them out singing. The crowd will love it. We can decorate the pillars with hieroglyphics. I know just the man to advise us. A scholar of antiquities, Mr. Bunbury. A young fellow, a bit dotty, but brilliant."

"If you don't mind my asking," Hugh said, "where did you, ah, dig him up?"

"I placed an ad in the *Times*."

"I see."

"Hugh, we have got to top Drury Lane on opening night and I know they haven't got an Egyptian sketch."

"How do you know that?" Daniel asked.

"I just do. They stole our nymph idea, by the way."

Daniel pondered that for a moment. "I might also ask how you came by that information."

Hugh shrugged. "Everybody does nymphs. Cheap

costume. Bit of gauze here and there, and you're done."

"Good Lord, Daniel, this is only theater. Not as if we are talking about secret naval intelligence or the movement of troops. We know what our competition is doing." Terence waved a hand. "It's in the air. More or less."

"Whatever you say, Terence." Daniel looked at the drawings. "How much will this cost, McNeel?"

The property master named a sum that made Lord York's eyes open wide.

"You must be joking."

"No, sir."

"We'll have to cut it, Terence. There is no money coming in."

"I beg to differ."

"Do not take that pompous tone with me."

Hugh and McNeel exchanged a glance and walked a little distance away.

"My dear brother-in-law," Terence began jovially. "Do you prefer this tone of voice? Shall I continue?"

Daniel scowled. "Pray, do."

"We have a new benefactor. Or perhaps I should say benefactress."

"And who would that be? Have you promised a starring role to some little tart with a noble lover? Does the tart sing and dance?"

"No, not exactly."

Lizzie Loudermilk entered the workshop and slammed the door behind her. "I heard there's to be a new sketch added. Am I in it?"

Terence turned to her. "No."

"Is the tart in it?"

"There is no tart."

"You *were* talking about a singing, dancing tart. I assume you didn't mean me."

"Of course not, Lizzie dear."

Lizzie put her hands on her hips and took a belligerent stance. "Is Terence telling the truth, my lord?"

"As far as I know," Daniel said. "But I am not at all sure about the tart part."

"I knew it," Lizzie growled. "Turn my back for one minute and someone else gets a plum role."

"But you will strain your voice if you sing any more songs," Terence said in a vain attempt to placate her. "There are seventeen enchanting new musical numbers in *The Shepherdess*. Who could ask for anything more?"

"Who could ask for anything more? There's a song in that," Hugh said to McNeel, who nodded.

Daniel held up a hand for silence. No one saw. "Quiet!" he roared.

"Oo! His lordship is roaring. Quiet, everyone," Lizzie said. "You roar quite nicely, Daniel."

"Thank you, Lizzie. There seems to be some confusion. Terence, you mentioned a benefactress. Who is this person?"

"A relation."

"One of yours, I suppose," Daniel said.

"Actually, Daniel, she is also your relation now. A cousin by marriage."

Lord York looked at him, aghast. "Oh, no. Not Penelope."

"Yes, Penelope. She is an amateur expert on hieroglyphics and has agreed to lend us her research materials on the subject. And ten thousand pounds."

"Ten thousand! We will be paid!" Hugh cried. He took McNeel's arm and they did a circular jig. "Money! Money! Money!"

Daniel held up a hand again. McNeel caught his eye and stopped.

"You said *lend*, Terence. Penelope is *lending* us her research materials and ten thousand pounds.

That means we have to pay it back. That is twice as much as what we already owe."

"But haven't the bills been paid, Daniel?" Terence gave him an innocent look worthy of a dewy-eyed ingenue.

"Yes, you fool! I paid them out of my own pocket. Of course, I had to use your rob-Peter-to-pay-Paul accounting methods to do it, but I did it! And we are not going to take on such a sizeable debt!"

"Let me explain," Terence began. "Oh, where to begin?"

"At the beginning," McNeel said sensibly.

"No, the end is easier," Terence replied. "You see, Daniel, I did not make myself clear. Penelope is going to *lend* us her research but she will *give* us the ten thousand pounds."

"Are you joking?"

"No. She said to tell you that she is grateful for all you have done for her."

"No need to explain everything, Terence," Daniel said hastily.

Penelope put on her spectacles and opened the first book. "Now, Mr. Bunbury. It indicates here that the hieroglyphic design you have in mind represents the amount of wheat in the pharaoh's granaries. Yet you say it represents the number of the pharaoh's concubines."

Mr. Bunbury looked over her shoulder. "You may be right. I think it is wheat. Perhaps I was looking at it upside down. That changes the meaning."

"So we agree," Penelope continued, "right side up is correct."

"Yes, unless we try it sideways."

"Mr. Bunbury!" Penelope looked fondly over

her spectacles at her fellow scholar of antiquities. "You know perfectly well what that means."

"Yes, my dear." He kissed her neck.

"We can't have that sort of thing onstage," she giggled.

"No, Penelope. It wouldn't be at all proper."

"Not at all."

Chapter Seventeen

Opening night . . .

As Terence had hoped, Lizzie Loudermilk's name upon the bill drew the crowds. He stood outside the theater with Lord York, watching a throng of people push and shove each other to get tickets for the pit.

The members of the *ton* entered in a more sedate fashion, allowing their liveried servants to do the pushing and shoving for them.

"It is a gratifying sight, is it not?" he said to Daniel.

"Yes, but it is an hour before the curtain rises. What will they do until then?"

"Throw orange peels at each other. Flirt. Gossip."

"I am very glad that your parents begged off. The Shys would think a riot like this most unseemly."

Terence laughed in an amiable way. "Yes, I believe they are still recovering from the news of your hasty marriage to my sister."

"They sent us a silver toasting fork."

"Useful."

"And five jars of gooseberry jam."

"Tasty."

Daniel sighed. "Mrs. Shy made it quite clear that it was difficult to procure good jam on such short notice."

"Mama rises to every challenge. Jo is like her in that way."

"Yes," Daniel said. "Where is Jo, by the way?"

"Backstage, helping Lizzie."

A bell rang and the shoving crowd surged through the doors.

"We must take our seats, Daniel. This is a great occasion. Think of it! Our first opening night. There will be many more."

"Perhaps."

They walked past the huge sign that advertised the bill and listed the principal performers.

"Now, let's see. Did Bert get it right? He has re-painted that damned sign so many times . . . yes, yes, it is correct," Terence said. "We are beginning with the Chamber of Wonders and the musical mummies."

"That set is dazzling. McNeel outdid himself."

"And we have Penelope and Mr. Bunbury to thank for its archeological accuracy. They worked far into the night together, puzzling over dusty tomes and hieroglyphic designs."

Daniel raised an eyebrow. "They seem to be quite fond of each other already."

"Well, you know how it is in the theater," Terence said breezily. "That sort of thing goes on all the time."

"Tell me, Terence," Daniel said. "Were you plan-ning—I mean, did you hope that your sister and I . . . Do you remember when you put us in that rosy light and told me to look into her eyes?"

"Yes. That was a magic moment, wasn't it? You never know what will happen when the light is right."

They came to a nondescript side door and entered the theater.

The audience was noisy, but they seemed to be enjoying themselves, even though nothing was happening. Terence and Daniel took their seats in the box.

"That's how we want 'em," Terence whispered. "Restive, but festive." He peered into the wings. "There is Tom. I think he's going to send a nymph out. I told him he might."

Daniel saw a girl in pink gauze and heavy make-up, and one of those awful wigs, waiting in the wings for her cue. And was that Jo? He caught a glimpse of a honey-haired woman in white dashing by in the darkness of the wings, but he could not be sure.

The nymph raised her tambourine and ran upon the stage, to wild applause. She pranced and pirouetted, then looked coyly over her shoulder, emitting squeaks of fear.

The cello players bowed a throbbing, ominous note in unison.

A satyr bounded upon the boards, roaring and thumping his chest. He pursued the nymph for several minutes, pretending to lose her while she was in plain sight, and looking out into the audience as if she had danced right over the heads of the louts in the pit.

The louts cheered and helped him out by pointing.

"She's over there, ye great booby!"

"In back of ye!"

The satyr turned around, threw his hands up in the air with joy, and gave his nymph a look of goggle-eyed lust. He caught her this time and threw her over his shoulder, exiting stage right with a jaunty wave. There was loud clapping and a few shouts of "Get on wif it!" and "Start the show!"

The great curtain shook a bit, in preparation for its rise, and the audience settled down. But only for a few seconds. There was thunderous applause as the curtain went up slowly, majestically, to reveal the Chamber of Wonders. Towering columns, decorated with palm-frond capitals and hieroglyphics that were too small to make out, dwarfed everything else on stage.

A stagehand, unseen by all save Terence and Daniel, pushed a final column into position.

"They weigh very little," Terence whispered. "Quite hollow, of course, made of battens and canvas. McNeel is most ingenious."

Daniel nodded. He had not seen the rehearsals for this act.

A row of sarcophagi, also decorated with hieroglyphics, moved forward as if pushed by some unseen giant hand. The orchestra struck up a wailing Arabian melody of dubious provenance, and the sarcophagus doors opened.

The bandaged mummies inside kept their eyes closed . . . and then stared solemnly at the delighted crowd. The screams were deafening.

"That Egyptian eye makeup is quite striking, don't you think?" Terence whispered.

"Yes," Daniel said, "but do be quiet."

"Why? No one else is."

"You have a point."

"*Let the auld bugger rest . . .*" the mummies sang. "*Let the auld bugger rest . . .*"

"Good Lord." Daniel rolled his eyes. "That is not one of Hugh's best tunes."

"The audience loves it," Terence said.

They were clapping, not in time, but enthusiastically, and singing along as best they could.

The mummies finished the song and stepped out upon the stage as the sarcophagi moved away, again as if by a giant unseen hand. They picked up their trailing bandages and began to dance, not very well, launching into another song.

"Wrap me in your arms and row me down the Nile . . ."

Daniel winced. "This one is worse."

Terence ignored him and leaned over the edge of the box, seeming thrilled by the commotion below and the spectacle onstage.

"Let it be over," Daniel said under his breath. "Please let it be over soon."

He sat up straighter and leaned to one side to look into the wings. That was Jo, by Ginny's side, pulling pins from the pincushion on Ginny's wrist and sewing up a nymph who had come undone. Ginny took the shears that hung around her neck and snipped here and there. The nymph ran off.

Jo looked up and caught Daniel's eye. Even from here, he could see how happy she was.

He did not mind, so long as she remained backstage. There were limits. He had reached his. The mummies were groaning out the chorus, over and over.

The curtain came down and the orchestra ceased playing. Terence leaned out of the box and attempted to communicate with the conductor by wild gestures. The conductor only shrugged.

Daniel heard a faint patter and looked down to see the rabble throwing orange peels and other fruit at the curtain. A nymph ran out to distract them and received a direct hit on the rump with a piece of peel.

"Good shot, Mick!" someone cried. "We loves you, miss!"

She took a bow and scampered into the wings again.

Daniel spotted something green at the top of the curtain. Green and yellow. A parrot. Molly's parrot.

The bird used its beak and claws to climb down the curtain. The audience did not notice at first, but when the parrot was halfway down, they did. They applauded, thinking it another diversion.

"Oh, no," Daniel whispered, "not Nippy."

Tom ran out, dressed in a gentleman's clothes. He bowed and stretched out a hand to the bird. "Presenting . . . Nippy! The winged wonder!"

Nippy turned his head, saw Tom's hand, and lived up to his name. Tom yelled and sucked his finger.

The crowd roared with laughter.

"Good bit!" Terence said. "We must keep that in. Make a note, Daniel."

Tom picked up a piece of tossed fruit and lured Nippy onto his shoulder. The parrot chuckled into his ear, obviously enjoying the attention. They strolled into the wings, as if the whole thing had been planned to perfection.

Lord York sank his head into his hands. "What next?"

"A brief interval," Terence said. "Come, let us go backstage and see if we can find my sister."

The audience resumed throwing orange peels at the curtain as the men went out the back door of the box. Their heels clattered upon the wrought iron staircase, unheard in the cacophony of scenery for the next act being dragged into place by shouting stagehands.

Terence saw Tom and shook his hand. "Good work, Tom!"

"Careful, sir. When Nippy bit my finger, I thought it was a goner. But it is still attached."

"Very good. Nice to have all five."

"Yes, sir. Have you seen Molly?"

"No."

"I wants to get this damned parrot off me shoulder. He'll take me ear off next."

Terence smoothed the bird's green plumage and scratched its head. "Nippy wouldn't do that, would you, Nippy?"

The parrot gave an evil chuckle.

"Have you seen Jo, Tom?"

"She was just over there." The stage manager pointed to a crowd of giggling nymphs that did not include Jo. "I don't know where she is now." He eased the parrot onto the side rigging and walked away. The backstage bell rang. "Places, everyone!" Tom called.

Terence, who had wandered off, dashed back to Daniel's side.

"Back to the box. We can't miss *The Shepherdess!*"

The great curtain shook a little and then went up again. A rustic set, bedecked with roses and peaches and other suggestive botanical touches, was greeted by the audience with scattered clapping and a few boos.

"Oh, dear," Terence said, "they don't seem to like this one as much. It is a little dreary. Perhaps a lamp or two is out. Make a note, Daniel."

Daniel ignored this request and concentrated on the stage.

After a few notes from a pan-pipe, Lizzie Loudermilk strolled on, her hands on her ample hips, trilling the first song for all she was worth. The house erupted with thunderous applause and shrieks of admiration.

"That's better," Terence said.

Daniel studied the set. There was a screen to one side of it, built to resemble a farmer's cottage and to hide the little satyr who was singing the blacksmith's part. One side of it, the side that faced away from the audience, was open, so that Fred could read the blacksmith's lips.

Harry Longwood came on and clasped Lizzie around the waist. He too burst into song, a full-throated bass melody of love. The crowd screamed for more. Lizzie threw them a flirty smile and leaned back on Harry's shoulder. They began their duet.

Terence breathed a sigh of relief. "Excellent. This is going splendidly."

Daniel knew that Fred was behind the screen. What he didn't know was that Jo was there, too, at Lizzie's insistence.

The Shepherdess had been divided into two parts, owing to the very large number of songs in it. Less than an hour later, they were well into the second part.

Jo held the music for Fred, turning the pages so that he would not miss a note.

"Thank'ee, miss," he whispered when Lizzie launched into her solo. He mopped his brow. " 'Tis hard work, singing for someone else."

"You are doing wonderfully well," Jo whispered back.

"Very tricky it is to look at him and look at the music."

"Yes."

He turned suddenly. "Harry's going to lift her. Here comes the roar."

Jo saw the mighty blacksmith lift up Lizzie and heard Fred let out a huge roar simultaneously.

"Perfect!" she whispered.

Fred drew in a deep breath and roared again, keeping his eye on Harry all the while. The song continued, with Lizzie slung over Harry's shoulder, trilling like a young girl. She was in fine voice, much to Jo's relief. Jo knew every word and note of *The Shepherdess*, and could sing it if she had to, but her glimpses of the crowd had terrified her.

The theater was packed. Every available seat on the pit benches was taken, and the boxes were filled. They loved their Lizzie.

Jo looked through the music to be ready for Harry's next song. Then she heard an odd noise . . . not a song. Not dialogue. A sheepish sort of noise. But it stopped. She assumed one of the stagehands was having a bit of fun and thought nothing more of it.

She did not see Tom and some members of the crew push a huge box on wheels to the other side of the wings. Busy with the music, Jo did not see him dismiss the stagehands and prepare to lift the side of the box straight up.

Lizzie didn't either.

The singer took center stage, held up her arms to her adoring public, and launched into her final solo.

Tom lifted the side. Several sheep ran onstage, *baaa*ing frantically. The audience howled with delight. The biggest sheep bumped the back of Lizzie's knees and she fell backwards over it, landing with a shriek unhurt on her bum. A lamb scampered over and licked her nose.

The crowd clapped and screamed for more.

Lizzie scrambled to her feet and pushed the lamb away. Its mother lowered her woolly head and butted Lizzie on the thigh.

She went down again, shrieking bloody murder.

Fred and Jo peeked out to see what was going on. She looked up and saw Daniel in the box, staring at her, horrified. His mouth was open. Terence was next to him, laughing hysterically.

Jo ducked back behind the screen.

"What's going on?" Fred whispered.

"I don't know," she whispered back.

"Why are we whispering? No one can hear nothing but Lizzie's screaming."

Harry Longwood was doing his best to rid the stage of sheep, but the baffled animals eluded his grasp.

Jo looked around the edge of the screen again. She could just see Tom Higgins, laughing his head off, sitting on top of a huge box filled with straw. One little lamb had gone back in.

"Tom is playing a prank! On Lizzie!"

The singer had apparently just realized the same thing.

"I'll rip your head off for this, Tom!" She tripped over another confused sheep to get to him. "Out of my way!"

There was more thunderous applause and laughter.

"Ow!" Lizzie's mouth opened wide to shriek again . . . but no sound came out. She had lost her voice.

The audience waited. Jo peeked out. There was nothing for it. She began to sing Lizzie's solo. The singer threw her a wild look but Lizzie was nothing if not a trouper. Her mouth formed every note but

Jo sang every one. Harry got behind Lizzie and clasped her waist, offering what support he could.

The sheep bumbled around the stage, testing the scenery for edibility. Lizzie ignored them and went right on performing. Fred held the music for Jo, but she knew the role too well to need it.

The second lamb kicked up its heels and headed straight for the screen. It bumped into it once . . . twice . . . and the screen came down.

Jo went right on singing.

Chapter Eighteen

Terence wiped away his tears of laughter and turned to Daniel. "That was wonderful! Absolutely wonderful! Were the sheep your idea?"

"No," Daniel said, "and seeing my blushing bride singing on stage was not my idea, either."

"Oh, don't be such a prig, Daniel," Terence said cheerfully. "Bit late in the day for that, eh?" He composed himself. "I must find out where the sheep came from."

"I suspect someone was playing a prank."

"You may be right, but who?"

"Ginny mentioned that Tom and Lizzie had quarreled. They were both at Derrydale, though he did not stay. I did not think much of it at the time. He may have hidden my sheep in the theater wagon and brought them back."

Terence snapped his fingers. "Of course! He did not bring back much furniture. What a glorious prank!"

The audience was still clapping.

"They loved it, that is clear. And they assume it's

all part of the show. The only question is, can we do it again?"

"If you pay me for the sheep."

Terence slapped him on the back. "Of course, my friend. We are rolling in money now, thanks to Penelope. Though you could let me have them for free. What are a few sheep between friends?"

Daniel got to his feet. "I must find Jo."

"Don't scold her, Daniel." Terence's tone was suddenly serious. "She did the right thing."

Lord York didn't answer. He left through the back door of the box and clattered down the wrought iron staircase once more. He pushed through the knots of sweating, laughing performers but could not find Jo.

He did see Molly, being sewn into her white costume by Ginny. A few feathers fluttered to the floor but she looked enough like a bird to please the waiting crowd.

Daniel searched for another few minutes and found Tom, still laughing. Wonder of wonders, Lizzie was laughing with him—silently. They sat atop the box, which seemed to be inhabited once more by complaining sheep.

"That was a good one, Tom," she said in a hoarse rasp. "But I *will* rip your head off, mark my words."

"Ye had it coming, Lizzie girl."

She could only croak. Whether she agreed or disagreed was not clear.

"Higgins!" Daniel said sternly.

The stage manager sat bolt upright and stopped laughing. "Yes, sir?"

"Were those my sheep?"

Tom hesitated and looked at Lizzie. "Yes, sir."

"Poaching is a hanging offense. You know that."

"I didn't poach 'em, sir. I borrowed 'em."

"I ought to sack you."

Lizzie climbed down off the box and came over. "You can't," she rasped. "The show is a hit. And our Tom seems to have a way with sheep."

"Please do not talk, Lizzie. The show will not be a hit if you cannot sing. Have you seen Jo?"

"No, but don't scold her. She saved my bacon, sir. Or should I say mutton?" Lizzie let out a wheezy laugh. "And she saved the show."

"Perhaps she did."

Daniel returned to the box. "Jo is nowhere to be found."

"She will turn up," Terence said.

"Not in the next act, I hope."

"No, this is *The Castaway.* Lizzie doesn't sing in it—Andy does. He is a baritone. Jo is a soprano."

"I know that, Terence. All of London knows."

Terence put a finger to his lips. The great curtain rose once more.

Jagged rocks bathed in blue light had been placed in the center of the stage. The wooden waves began to roll.

"Nice effect. Good guano," Terence murmured.

Andy, the castaway, clambered over the top of the rock and sang of his loneliness. A few of the more sentimental members of the audience took out their handkerchiefs and sobbed noisily during the quietest parts.

"What ho!" Andy said when he had finished the first song. "Yon bird doth fly! Oh, yon bird!"

"I do hope it's not Nippy," Daniel said dryly.

There was a faint clink from the stage rigging and Molly sailed into view, flying out over the first rows to gasps and wild applause. She sailed back, circling over Andy's head.

"Hope!" the lonely castaway cried. "Hope is the thing with feathers!"

Molly lost a few. They drifted down upon the rocks. She sailed out again, smiling and waving to the audience.

Terence frowned. "She mustn't wave. Make a note, Daniel."

They heard a louder clink and then a clank from the rigging that held the backdrops.

"Wait a minute. We don't change drops for this scene," Terence said.

Another backdrop came down with lightning speed. It was the battleship with blazing cannons. Molly was headed straight for it. She went right through, kicking her legs wildly. "Help!"

"That is one of the old ones we got from those damned Italians! The canvas must be half-rotten or she wouldn't have gone through!"

"The audience seems to like it even better than the sheep," Daniel said.

Molly swung back out. "Ow! Help!"

The crowd cheered and clapped. Molly smiled and waved as her swings on the wire shortened. Andy sat on his rock and waved too.

Terence got to his feet. "It is time to put a stop to this."

Tom had Signor Arlecchino in a hammerlock hold by the time Terence and Daniel got backstage. "I have him, sir!"

"Explain yourself, Arlecchino," Terence said.

"Ye won't understand him if he does, sir," Tom grumbled.

But to everyone's amazement, the struggling fellow answered without an accent. "He's . . . choking me! Can't . . . explain . . . if he's choking me!"

"Let him go, Tom."

Arlecchino coughed. "I am with the Drury Lane players."

"He was a-spying on us and a-sabotaging our show, sir. He decided to confess."

"Aye, after you punched me."

"He was the one what drilled the holes in the roof and made the leaks," Tom went on. "He painted bears and dogs on *The Shepherdess* backdrop. He led our Molly astray."

Daniel folded his arms across his chest. "I see. Terence, what shall we do?"

Terence studied the little man and paced up and down. "What is your real name?"

"John Arly. Close enough to Arlecchino, don't you think?"

"You had us all fooled."

Arly grinned.

Terence walked back to Daniel. "There is only one thing we can do."

"And what is that?"

" Ask the man to work for us."

"The idea is insane," Daniel said severely. "Like everything else that happens around here. No doubt I will eventually go insane myself."

"Quite right," Terence said cheerfully, not really listening at all.

Daniel found Jo at last. She was sitting on the sheep box and feeding the animals bits of hay from *The Shepherdess* scenery, which had been pushed into the wings.

She looked up. "Hello."

"Hello."

"Why the long face? Opening night was a howling success, Daniel."

"So it was," he said gloomily. "I now have a performing wife. And performing sheep."

"They were very good, were they not?" she said, sticking another bit of hay through a crack. "Real troupers, Tom said."

"I have had a word with Tom, and I shall have another."

"Don't scold him, Daniel. What's done is done. And don't scold me."

He picked up a stalk of hay and thrust it through a knothole. A pair of sheepy lips took it eagerly. "I wasn't going to. You did the right thing."

"Do you mean to say that you are not angry? I was onstage. All of London saw me."

"No one will remember anything but the pratfalls. And Lizzie. And the sheep."

She patted the box. "Poor things. They are very sweet."

He sat down beside her.

"What are you thinking, Daniel?"

"That I . . . I love you. No matter what happens."

"That's a good start." She kissed him.

He kissed her back.

"That's even better."

More Regency Romance
From Zebra

Discover the Romances of
Hannah Howell

More Historical Romance From
Jo Ann Ferguson

Available Wherever Books Are Sold!

Visit our website at **www.kensingtonbooks.com**.

Embrace the Romance of
Shannon Drake

When We Touch
0-8217-7547-2 $6.99US/$9.99CAN

The Lion in Glory
0-8217-7287-2 $6.99US/$9.99CAN

Knight Triumphant
0-8217-6928-6 $6.99US/$9.99CAN

Seize the Dawn
0-8217-6773-9 $6.99US/$8.99CAN

Come the Morning
0-8217-6471-3 $6.99US/$8.99CAN

Conquer the Night
0-8217-6639-2 $6.99US/$8.99CAN

The King's Pleasure
0-8217-5857-8 $6.50US/$8.00CAN

Available Wherever Books Are Sold!

Visit our website at **www.kensingtonbooks.com.**